JONAH'S MIRROR

by the same author

AN ASH-BLONDE WITCH
FULL MOON
SELKIE
ISABEL'S DOUBLE
WHAT BECKONING GHOST?
YOUNG MAN OF MORNING

for younger children

THE HALLOWE'EN CAT

JONAH'S MIRROR

Kenneth Lillington

faber and faber

LONDON · BOSTON

First published in 1988
by Faber and Faber Limited
3 Queen Square London WC1N 3AU

Photoset by Parker Typesetting Service Leicester
Printed in Great Britain by
Richard Clay Ltd Bungay Suffolk
All rights reserved

British Library Cataloguing in Publication Data
Lillington, Kenneth
Jonah's mirror
I. Title
823'.914[J]   PZ7

ISBN 0-571-14961-8

For Simon Choat

CHAPTER ONE

Jonah Sprockett became rich and famous early in life, mainly on the strength of his three great inventions, the bossle wheel, the knubbing cleat (which superseded the micro chip), and, of course, the sprockett hasp, which made his name a household word.

Was he happy? For years he was too busy to think about it. To become a millionaire while still young involves a lot of sacrifice. Jonah went without pastimes, friends, alcohol, tobacco and even sleep. He was a simple man, and asked little of life, except to make money hand over fist. But eventually it occurred to him that no, he was not happy, he was not happy at all; in fact he was depressed; in fact he was profoundly, abysmally depressed. He went to a psychiatrist.

'You die if you worry, you die if you don't,' said the psychiatrist cordially, 'so why worry at all?'

'I am not worried. I am depressed.'

'Ah. That may present something of a problem. I could give you tablets to cure your depression, but they may have the side effect of causing hysteria, and then you would need anti-hysteria tablets, which might re-establish depression.'

'Oh.'

'However, there is a possible cure, which in the profession we call Phase Three, or Perfect Equipoise. How can I explain this to a layman? . . . Imagine a pendulum brought to rest, stilled between its poles . . . The treatment? Take no tablets of either kind. Abstain completely. Simply breathe deeply and regularly . . . Yes, in most cases, highly effective, but of course it would cost a little more . . .'

'But I could do that without coming to you at all.'

The psychiatrist perceived that his client was of above average intelligence, and changed his approach. 'Well,' he said, 'the trouble may lie in your infancy. Did your parents hate you? You have a most ridiculous name. Jonah stands for jinx, or hoodoo. Perhaps they named you this out of spite?'

'No they didn't. They were devoted parents,' said Jonah resentfully. 'They were film actors. When I was on the way, my father had a part in a great screen epic called *Jonah and the Whale*, and they named me Jonah for luck.'

'I see,' said the psychiatrist, wrinkling his brows. Expensive minutes went by.

'I just want taking out of myself,' said Jonah desperately.

'Ah! Then join an amateur dramatic society!'

'Why?'

'As an actor you really do become someone else – Hamlet or Charley's Aunt or a character in one of these modern plays who's buried up to his neck in earth – '

'Flowerpot men?'

'You've got the idea,' said the psychiatrist cheerfully. 'Try it out, Mr Sprockett. See you next Monday?'

So Jonah did join the Ambleford Players, but not to play Hamlet or anything else, for they quickly discovered that, even if he were not the worst actor in the world, he would certainly get into the medal tables. They did, however, put him in charge of lighting and stage effects. Their hall was too low for them to 'fly' their scenery, and they could not afford a revolving stage, and his inventive genius was invaluable. They were rehearsing a Christmas pantomime, *Cinderella*, and he worked out a most wonderful device for this. Where the fairy godmother waved her wand, and Cinderella changed from rags to a beautiful ball-dress, he fixed it so that she was transformed on the spot, pouf! Like that! Marvellous!

It was really quite simple. He did it with mirrors; more exactly, one mirror. All that happened was that two girls walked on to the stage holding the beautiful dress and popped it over Cinderella's head, sweet as a nut, and because of the way Jonah had fixed his mirror, the audience couldn't see them do it! Then he would shift the mirror slightly, and there was Cinderella looking like the fairy on the Christmas tree! It worked several times in rehearsal, the cast was delighted, and Jonah felt slightly less depressed.

The first night arrived, the pantomime got under way, and the two girls walked on from the wings carrying the dress. But something had gone wrong. Cinderella had vanished.

These two girls had fine stage presence. They signalled for the curtain to be lowered, walked out front and sang a duet, all so neatly that the audience didn't know anything had gone wrong, and by the time they'd finished their song Cinderella had reappeared. Where had she been? Why, nowhere. She had been standing there all the time, astounded by the behaviour of her fellow actresses. Vanished? What did they mean, vanished? But she was a good trouper too, she went on with her act, and the performance ran smoothly to its end.

But there was a curious after-effect. The girl who had played Cinderella found that she had become left-handed. To *be* left-handed is no handicap, but it is disconcerting to find yourself so after you've been right-handed all your life. She became clumsy and inept. She kept colliding with things and failing to grasp what she reached for. To get an idea of this, look into the side mirror of your dressing-table and try to pat your hair into shape. You'll find your hand straying all over the place. But don't let anyone see you at it, or they'll think you've gone mad.

She nearly had a breakdown, and declared that if Jonah were to stay on with the company, she would leave. The others backed her up, and Jonah was dismissed. He was most upset. There were some pretty girls in the company, and he had dared to hope that one of them might take a liking to him, preferably Cinderella herself, who in her ball-dress was just like the girl of his dreams. Had she known that he was a millionaire and famous, she might have felt differently, but Jonah wanted to be loved for himself alone, and was working incognito, having ingeniously changed his name to Joshua Sproggett, and as such he didn't rate with the hard-hearted beauty, who in daily life was a traffic warden. He took his mirror and departed more depressed than ever. 'Lonely to my grave, I suppose,' he lamented. Of course, there was always his fiancée, Miss Wingbone, but still – Miss Wingbone!

Jonah came into his office carrying *The Times*, folded over at the crossword.

'How weary, stale, flat and unprofitable,' he said to Miss Wingbone, who was also his co-director, 'seem to me all the uses of this world.'

'Yes, especially unprofitable,' she replied grimly. 'Seen our books lately?'

4

She was Miss Wingbone to everybody, including herself. Jonah got over the awkwardness of this by never calling her anything. Work being slack, she spent much of her time knitting. Although arguably the cleverest woman in the world, she was not a skilled knitter, and could manage nothing more ambitious than a 'long thing', which had begun as a scarf, but now fell in many coils round her feet.

Jonah did not answer her question. Whenever the conversation got awkward, he would revert to *The Times* crossword.

'Beatrix Potter's mad relation, six letters,' he said. He twisted his long, lean body into the shape of a monkey puzzle tree and repeated in an agonized voice, 'Beatrix Potter's mad relation . . . ?'

'Nutkin,' said Miss Wingbone without hesitation. 'Look, people keep asking for you and the secretaries are running out of excuses. "I'm sorry, Mr Sprockett can't see you just now, as he is busy growing a beard." Rather lame, isn't it?'

'This vehicle's a stuffy one, nine letters. An anagram, perhaps?'

'No. "Stuffy one" would make either *Festufony* or *Yofenstuf*, both of which are nonsense. The answer is *taxidermy*. Look, the manageress of Kitchen Supplies has just rung up from our Leeds office. She's beefing about our latest dishwasher. She says it flings things against the opposite wall. She thinks we must have crossed it with a circular saw. She compares it to a madman dealing a hand of cards.'

'Deluded creature.'

'She seemed lucid enough to me, just exasperated, and possessed of a certain flair for imagery.'

'Does she suppose that to have a stack of clean crockery would make anyone the least bit happier in this loathsome world?'

'Yes, I should think she probably does.'

'False,' said Jonah, dropping limply into a chair. 'False.'

'You really are in a state, aren't you?' said Miss Wingbone curiously. 'Isn't the dram. soc. work going too well?'

Jonah told her about Cinderella.

'The girl's clearly a fool,' said Miss Wingbone. 'That mirror sounds interesting.'

He showed it to her that evening in his flat. It was an oblong sheet of glass hanging, apparently without support, inside a chromium frame some six inches wider than itself all round.

Miss Wingbone ran her finger all round the space between mirror and frame. 'Very neat,' she commented. 'It's held in place by magnetism, obviously. What's this little wheel for?'

Jonah demonstrated. As he moved the small, milled wheel on the righthand side of the frame, the mirror turned inside it till its edge presented itself to him. He moved the wheel the other way, and the movement was reversed.

'The principle is elementary,' he remarked while doing so. 'Anyone who understands cosines – '

'Don't look now,' said Miss Wingbone, 'but you've vanished.'

'Vanished?'

'Yes. Very clever. But please reappear.'

'This is absurd,' said Jonah. Looking down at his body, he saw himself perfectly well, but his reflection in the mirror had gone. Miss Wingbone was standing just behind him. He reached out a hand to touch her. But he could not. His hand strayed past her face, as if following a track of its own. He tried the other hand. It, too, moved deliberately away, like a ball on a bagatelle board following its groove.

6

'It's all right,' he commanded. 'Don't panic.'

'I am not panicking,' said Miss Wingbone, 'but I don't like being engaged to a disembodied voice. Please reappear.'

'It's a bit tricky, that's all,' muttered Jonah.

He moved the mirror this way and that, fingering the little wheel delicately. It was like dialling a foreign station on the radio. Once or twice he saw himself for a fleeting second, as if a giant's thumb had flicked him across the glass. And then, click! the mirror came round full face and he reappeared in it, large as life.

'Welcome back,' said Miss Wingbone.

'Trick of the light,' said Jonah, shaking his head bemusedly.

'Well, yes. But let me know when you're going to do it again.'

Jonah took his mirror home to his luxury flat in an estate in the Surrey hills, stood it at the end of his bedroom, facing the window, and went to bed. The moonlight, reflected from it, formed a phantom parallelogram on his window curtains.

Normally, he dreamed so seldom that he sometimes wondered if he had a deficient unconscious mind. But tonight he did dream, in fitful fragments. They flashed like slides projected on a screen but removed too quickly for the eye to follow. He failed, with a pang of loss, to retain a single one. It was most tantalizing, this kaleidoscope of dreams, because each flash brought with it a pang of beauty more intense than anything in his waking experience.

He woke up, and sat up. Now here was a strange thing. The area of his windows had gone completely black, and the block of moonlight, reflected from the mirror, had become a door. He slipped from his bed and began walking slowly towards it. The door was almost closed, showing just a crack of light, but as he approached it, it gradually opened, like the automatic door in the supermarket. When he reached the doorway, he gazed out on a scene that made him catch his breath in wonder.

It reminded him of the fairy tales which his mother had read him in his infancy. He saw distant hills crowned with many-turreted palaces which gleamed like ivory in the moonlight. He saw, right below him, a valley full of flowering bushes, hueless in the dark, and, trickling down the hillside to his left, the quicksilver thread of a stream. He followed the course of this with his eyes to where it ran into a pool like an opal, and as he gazed, a silver unicorn came out of the shadows and drank.

It was December in his world, but here it seemed a lovely summer night, and the air was deliciously fragrant. He gazed and gazed in rapture. The unicorn finished drinking and trotted daintily out of sight. There was a disturbance in the bushes only a yard or two down the slope before him, and a girl emerged into view.

She wore a long russet gown with a green girdle, and sandals on her feet. The moonlight revealed her to be of inexpressible beauty, with a face and figure that made Cinderella in the pantomime seem like a rag doll. Long waves of golden hair cascaded down her back and rippled over her shoulders. In contrast to her simple dress, she wore on her head a small and scintillating crown.

She saw Jonah as soon as he saw her, and with a small cry of joy she climbed the slope towards him. She reached out to him eagerly. He stretched out his hand in response. They were within touching distance now,

8

and the nearness of her loveliness fairly stunned him. But it was as it had been when he had tried to reach Miss Wingbone after vanishing: their hands strayed apart, turned off, wandered. The joy faded from the girl's face.

Jonah always thought in mathematical terms. 'Vertical as well as horizontal movement, of course,' he muttered to himself. 'It should roll like a surfboard on a wave.' He motioned to the girl to wait and turned back to his mirror. Impossible to make the alterations here and now, of course. In impotent distress he fingered the serrated wheel and turned the mirror very slightly. At which the cloud-capped towers, the gorgeous palaces, yea the glamorous girl herself, faded, leaving not a wrack behind, unless you counted Jonah's windows.

CHAPTER TWO

'A dream, of course,' said Miss Wingbone.

'No, I had stopped dreaming and woken up,' replied Jonah, in his precise way. 'What I am telling you happened when I was fully conscious. My conclusion is that I entered a parallel universe.'

His tone was as matter-of-fact as if he had said, 'I took the M25 for Dorking.' Miss Wingbone smiled indulgently.

'Parallel universes are only a fancy.'

'Not any more,' said Jonah patiently, 'because I have now entered one.'

'Oh well,' said Miss Wingbone, still indulgently, 'tell me more. You were looking down into a valley?'

But when the girl entered the story, she tightened her lips.

'I don't like the sound of this. I'm not particularly religious, but I do agree with people who say that there's a wall between us and the next world, and that we aren't meant to break through it.'

'But I've done so, meant or not.'

'Well, don't go back again. This is no time to go gallivanting about alien universes. Think of Sprockett's Electricals. Yes, please do think of them. Do you know we're down to our last few million? You must get rid of that mirror.'

'I don't think anyone would want to buy it, and I can't see leaving it out for the dustman.'

'Give it to the university. To the Department of Science.'

'They couldn't make head or tail of it!'

'No, but they could write theses and run courses on it. They'd give you an honorary doctorate.'

'What about this wall, then? Suppose they break through it?'

'They must take that risk,' said Miss Wingbone indifferently.

Jonah took from his pocket a page torn from *The Times* and took refuge in the crossword.

'Hounded hound, eight letters.' His face crisped with anguish. 'Hounded *hound*? *Hound*ed hound?'

'Dogsbody,' said Miss Wingbone impatiently. 'What about that mirror?'

He gave in, as he had known he would. 'All right,' he sighed.

'You agree? Good. We'll take it to them now.'

'They're on their Christmas vacation.'

'There are residential holiday courses. Someone will be there. We'll go now.'

'At this time of night?'

'No time like the present. We'll leave it at Enquiries and you can send a letter of explanation.'

They carried the mirror out between them and put it in his car. The university stood on a hill amid acres of countryside. It was a cluster of buildings of depressing ugliness, like so many coal bunkers and rat traps, but Miss Wingbone was right, there was life there, for lights could be seen, showing through the hazy air in ragged blotches the colour of fox fur. A road for vehicles ran round the periphery, so that one could drive to the very door of the Enquiry Office. That is, in normal times one could; but just beyond the Visitors' Car Park, a good quarter of a mile away, the road was up for repair.

'That does it,' said Jonah.

'No it doesn't. Park in the car park and we'll carry it down the pedestrians' footpath.'

'It will be a hell of a walk with that thing.'

'We'll rest at intervals.'

Jonah parked the car and they began carrying the mirror down the footpath. What a weight! He had made the base very solid. They stopped every few yards.

'Oh, let's give this up and take it back.'

'It'll be worse going uphill. We've come a fair distance. Come on.'

A blob of moisture fell on Jonah's hand.

'It's going to rain.'

'We'll beat it if we hurry.'

It was unusually sultry for the time of the year and by now the air had become leaden. A thunderstorm in December is uncommon, and as the present writer has no knowledge of meteorology he cannot explain it. It is, however, a fact that lightning flickered like a snake's tongue, and was followed by a tremendous clap of thunder. The lightning became vicious and the thunder was an incessant bombardment. The rain-cloud burst and rain leaped down the hill. Down below, somewhere within the coal bunkers and rat traps, the Professor of Philosophy was giving an evening lecture on Illusion and Reality, and explaining that what we think we see and hear is really a state of mind. He frowned at the interruption and went on talking. But Jonah gasped 'Back to the car!'

They abandoned the mirror and stumbled up the path into the fury of the rain. They had gone only a few yards when the whole world behind them became a sheet of white fire. Miss Wingbone saw Jonah like a

12

photographic negative, white-haired and black in the face. He then vanished like a pricked bubble.

'Jonah?' she cried. For once in her life she became excited.

'*Jonah*! JONAH!!' Her cool, dry voice rose and cracked; she sounded like some demented prophetess of doom. There was no response.

She now went courageously through the roaring downpour to the mirror, with the vague thought of working the serrated wheel to some effect, but the chromium frame was vivid with electricity and pulsating like a neon sign, and to touch it would be fatal. She battled her way back to the car. Jonah had locked it and taken the keys. Mercifully, the rain slackened. Miss Wingbone strode from the university to the railway station, a daunting distance on foot, and caught a train back to her own dwelling. Jonah's mirror stood by the footpath where she had left it, its face lighting up with fiendish exultation.

Jonah's first sensation was that he was over-warm, for he was dressed for winter, and here it was summer. The university buildings, the cars in the park, were gone, of course. He was transported. With sudden curiosity he looked up the slope on which he stood to see whether the door was there, the door through which he had seen this very place the previous night; but there was no door, nor any building near at hand, although far off, across the valley, he could see the summits of the palaces. He looked along the tinkling stream to the pool below, wondering whether the unicorn would come again, but it did not. Nor would the girl, he thought sadly. Upon which she emerged from behind a bush, still wearing her russet gown, her sandals and her crown. She addressed him in these words:

> Master, I kissed the tiger-coloured stone
> To bring you to me; and last night you came,
> But proffering my hand to welcome you,
> I found it obstinately drawn aside
> As by some contrary magnetic force
> And shortly afterwards you vanished. Say,
> Now you return here, have you come to stay?

'Excuse me,' said Jonah humbly and respectfully, much as one might say to a lady, 'your slip is showing', 'but you are speaking in blank verse.'

'Forsooth, so I am,' said the girl, raising her hand to her mouth, 'with a rhyming couplet at the end, withal. We may sometimes speak in blank verse in court – no doubt you wot of it. But if I am to pass for a peasant girl, I must avoid it for the nones! It would let ye cat out of ye bag, would it not?'

'I'm sure it would,' said Jonah, and added, in a meek and deferential voice, 'and if I may say so, it would be a good idea to take your crown off, too.'

'Verily, it would,' said the girl, and took off her crown, swinging it schoolgirlishly by her side. 'Beshrew me, that was careless.'

'A princess, are you?' asked Jonah wonderingly.

'But of course. Surely you wot as much? I supposed you would wot everything about me.'

'Please,' said Jonah, quite dazed, 'what country is this?'

'In good sooth,' said the girl, looking at him in amazement, 'this is Sudonia.'

'Pardon me, your highness, what is your name?'

'I am the Princess Miranda. You seem to be in a state of acute wotlessness.'

'Please – with great respect – why should you expect me to know these things?'

'Well, really,' said the girl, 'since you have come to champion me and slay my foes, and release my father from his fatal Bond, I should have thought you'd have been told them.'

'I was summoned,' said Jonah, 'at very short notice.'

'Then I had better explain. Herkneth.'

Jonah took 'herkneth' to mean 'listen', and listened.

Miss Wingbone sensibly had a hot bath and changed her clothes, and then rang Jonah's flat. Receiving no reply, she got out her own car and drove back to the university. That mirror must not fall into anyone else's hands. Heaven knew what complications might follow if it did.

The rain had stopped, but it was still a miserable night, and the footpath was deserted. Torch in hand, she made her way to the mirror. Alas, the lightning had wrecked it. The sheet of glass, unbroken, lay on its face on the grass, no longer held in balance by the magnetism of the frame, and the frame itself was so buckled that it looked fit only to be slung away in some back yard in the company of old tin baths and stinging nettles. She twiddled the serrated wheel. It came off in her hand.

She paced about, shining her torch here and there, looking for Jonah's body. Within all reasonable radius, there was no body.

With some difficulty she carried the sheet of glass to her car. She returned for the buckled frame. In the privacy of her flat she studied the wreckage and meditated.

If Jonah had merely been struck by lightning, there

would surely be some signs of his remains – a smoking heap of bones, perhaps, with some charred remnants of his clothes. There were none. He seemed to have vanished from the face of the earth. From the face of the earth?

The lightning had struck the mirror, not Jonah. Was it possible that he had been precipitated into another universe by some cosmic accident? Oh, but surely not the one he had been describing? Fairy castles? A unicorn? A princess with a crown? It all sounded too near to the imaginings of our own world.

Yet Jonah was a strictly truthful young man, and not fanciful, having read nothing but technological books since the age of ten. If he had really been transported to such a place, an innocent like him, he might be in grave danger, especially if he had anything to do with that girl, of whom Miss Wingbone emphatically did not like the sound. Jonah's relationship with herself was purely intellectual, but he did sometimes show signs of susceptibility to quite unworthy females, and who could say into what perils some simpering mediaeval schemer in a coronet might lead him? There would presumably be no *Times* crossword in the other world and he would be at a loss how to amuse himself; but not, thought Miss Wingbone, frowning, not, perhaps, for long . . .

She would almost have preferred him to be a smoking heap of bones than in such a plight. It was her duty to rescue him, both from the parallel universe and from himself.

She took off her spectacles and instantly became a beautiful woman, but she was quite unaware of this, as she never gave any thought to her own appearance. She studied the mirror, and chewed the side-piece of her spectacles ruminatively.

She did not have Jonah's inventive genius, but for

grasping already established ideas she had no equal. She examined the mirror. It was a plain sheet, such as you might put on your wall. No, it was slightly concave. Or was it convex? As with so many things in this world, it depended on how you looked at it.

She examined the frame. She found some paper and began to make notes, replacing her spectacles. Lights glinted from their big round lenses.

Being quick on the uptake, Jonah soon mastered Miranda's vocabulary, and found her story easy to follow. Her father, the Good King Bevis, had one weakness: he was an incorrigible gambler. He was also fatally unlucky; if he backed a falcon it would manage to get itself tangled up in a tree, and if he backed a greyhound it would do its best and come in ninth. As a result he fell hopelessly into debt, chiefly to False Sir Topas, to whom he owed all his money and most of his worldly goods. As a desperate last resort he had wagered his own daughter, the Princess Miranda herself. So now Miranda was committed to marrying False Sir Topas, who would in the course of time become a Bad King, probably quite early, as Bevis would soon die of a broken heart.

'And you don't want to marry Sir Topas?' asked Jonah.

'Gramercy no! He is false.'

'Yes, of course,' said Jonah. He liked the way people were identified in this tale. As a little boy, when shown pictures of battles, he would ask his father, 'Which are the good people and which are the bad?', and when his father, like a man of good reason, would reply that there were faults on both sides, he would grow angry and thump him with his fists. In Miranda's country he would have been given a straight answer.

Although her father was a born loser, Miranda doubted whether all the wagers had been fair. False Sir Topas was in league with the court magicians, and it was highly likely that they had fixed things, as often as not.

'Are all the magicians Bad?' asked Jonah.

'Well demanded, sir,' replied Miranda, smiling. 'My tale provokes that question.' Yes, all the magicians were Bad, with one exception, Mad Waldo, who was good, but, as the name suggested, mad. He had once been a court magician himself, but he had taken to making insane predictions, such as that carriages would one day run without horses, and that people would be able to talk to one another over vast distances; and his fellow magicians, a very strong union, threw him out; and now he lived in a hut in the forest, where he spent his time giggling to himself and playing with bits of glass and wire.

'And yet, ofttimes,' remarked Miranda, 'mad people hit on truths which are beyond the reach of sane ones.' It seemed that the local peasants had great faith in Mad Waldo as a healer, and when their maladies developed complications would go to him for simples. He also had a wonderful gift for telling the future, and could easily have named the winners of races, if, of course, he had not been Good.

'I suspect, your highness,' suggested Jonah, 'that you have been to him yourself?'

He imagined that Miranda, under the cover of darkness, blushed. Yes, she had been to Mad Waldo. It had not been easy, for the spies of False Sir Topas watched her every move, but she had pretended to be visiting the poor, and had managed to make a call.

'It was this, noble sir,' she told Jonah, 'that led me to

18

you. I take it,' she added anxiously, 'that you *are* noble?
A prince? Or at least some great captain or chief? Since
you are disguised as a churl, it is difficult to tell.'

Jonah was wearing his expensive sheepskin coat, but
he did not protest. He decided that as he was chief of
Sprockett's Electricals, and might also be called a captain of industry, he could truthfully reply, 'Yes: I am
both a great captain and a chief. But how did this Waldo
lead you to me?'

'Did I not kiss the tiger-coloured stone?' replied
Miranda. She took a few moments to prevent herself
from speaking blank verse again. Jonah gathered that
the tiger-coloured stone was some bit of gimmickry in
Mad Waldo's hut, and that she had been persuaded to
kiss it 'at a certain hour on a certain night'.

'Tonight?'

'Even so.'

If she kissed the stone at the right moment, a great
captain or prince from a far distant land would come to
her by night. He would have magic powers of immense
resource. He would champion her cause, outwit False
Sir Topas, and slay her foes.

'Are there many of them?' asked Jonah apprehensively. He was conscious that he was carrying no better
weapon than a bunch of car keys.

'I ween there are some scores,' replied Miranda,
'because False Sir Topas is rich, and money talketh.'

'Haven't you got any friends?'

There was one, a young squire named Hubert. He
had first seen Miranda when she was dancing with
some of her ladies in a meadow. He had turned deathly
pale, and had said to his followers, 'Take me unto that
maiden, for sooth to say, I am half dead for love of her.'
He had then fallen into a swoon, in which he had
remained for two years.

'We can't exactly count on him, then.'

'Verily, sir, I count on you. Are you not my champion?'

This was very gratifying, because Jonah's feelings for Miranda were much akin to those of the Squire Hubert; but you had to be practical. Scores of foes? Armed with halberds, doubtless, and spiked metal balls on chains. He couldn't opt out like Hubert and swoon for two years. Miranda expected action.

'You're sure Mad Waldo hasn't got it wrong?' he asked tentatively.

'But it has all come to pass as foretold!'

'Yes, so it has,' muttered Jonah. 'New readers begin here.'

CHAPTER THREE

Miss Wingbone found Jonah's mirror easy to redesign: too easy, in fact. She could not imagine how such a simple mechanism could have such remarkable powers. She drew it in three sections, and gave each section to a different engineer, because, if one man constructed the whole thing and accidentally made himself vanish, it would be disastrous. When the sections were completed, she would assemble them herself.

But then what? Jonah had made the mirror solely to render Cinderella invisible to a theatre audience. All the rest had happened by accident. What was more, for anyone to enter the other world properly (always assuming that it existed) it seemed necessary for the mirror to be struck by lightning. Lightning never struck twice in the same place, did it? Or was that an old wives' tale? Anyway, what was one supposed to do, wait for the next storm?

She entered her sumptuous office and, for want of any work, took out the Long Thing and knitted a few more rows. There was enough of it now to swaddle her from head to foot like a mummy.

She put it aside and took a stroll round the outer office. Julie, the typist, was typing like a mad girl, her tongue sticking out and her hair falling about her face. She ripped the sheet of paper from her machine when

Miss Wingbone approached, but Miss Wingbone retrieved it from the wastepaper basket and read it. It contained one statement typed twenty times, with slight variations. 'The quick brown fox jimps over the laxy dof.' Miss Wingbone patted Julie on the head. 'Serves the laxy dof right,' she remarked and passed on. She was sorry for Julie, poor kid, having to pretend to work for fear of the sack.

In a secluded corner she came upon Peacock, the junior clerk. She felt even sorrier for him; he was so pathetically a square peg. He, too, was writing furiously. He, too, tried to hide what he was writing. Miss Wingbone took it from him and read: *'I entered the murky grounds of the sinister house. The air was ominous, foreboding, and laden with doom. The windows were eyeless sockets, and in the grim front door the letter box was like the obscene gash of a mouth. In the glare of the lamplight, yellow . . .'*

'Peacock,' chided Miss Wingbone gently, 'the glare of the lamplight, yellow, has nothing to do with the case. I know that you're taking a course in story-writing, but you must keep it to outside office hours. Have you no work to do?'

'No, Miss Wingbone.'

'And even if you had, this would be more real to you than Sprockett's Electricals, wouldn't it?'

'Yes, Miss Wingbone,' said Peacock helplessly.

Miss Wingbone had an extraordinary reaction. She wanted to take Peacock in her arms and mother him. She repressed the impulse sternly.

And then, just for a fleeting second, she had the slightest, slightest glimmer of understanding of what might have happened to Jonah. It was just the ghost of a hunch, without sense, without logic. And, like Jonah's dreams of two nights back, it was instantly gone beyond recall.

'It's a pity you can't knit,' she remarked. 'You could help me, one working at each end.'

Back in her office, she took out *The Times* crossword, which she could usually complete in about three minutes, but it bored her and she put it aside.

Julie and Peacock. She was only a few years older than they. What did they think of her? Neither as old nor young. She was just the dreaded Miss Wingbone. Suddenly she was near to tears. She frowned and pulled herself together. 'I must find Jonah's spare keys and take his car back,' she said to herself.

Miranda rose and shook back her golden hair.

'When day breaks, noble sir, will you challenge my father's foes, and throw yourself where their ranks are thickest?'

She was too innocent, this charming creature. 'We must be more subtle than that, Princess,' said Jonah. 'First I should like to meet Mad Waldo.'

'Wherefore wish you so?' asked Miranda dubiously.

'I may have something in common with him.'

'With a mad wizard?' Miranda sounded more dubious still. She rallied slightly. 'Pray, sir, what name shall I call you?'

'Jonah Sprockett.'

'Jonah Sprockett. Verily, it trippeth well off the tongue,' said Miranda politely, but with little conviction. Her champion was not quite what she had expected. 'If we are to meet Mad Waldo, it must be under the cloak of night.'

She beckoned for Jonah to follow, and led him down the grassy slope towards the woods. He had little idea of what was expected of him, and less still of how to go about it, but in the course of inventing the bossle wheel, the knubbing cleat and the sprockett hasp, not to mention trying to do *The Times* crossword, he had learned that it never helps to worry in advance about a problem. Go on in blind faith, and inspiration may visit you.

As they reached the woods he recalled that old saying, 'The grass is always greener on the other side'. It was as true of Sudonia as of his own world. Sudonia from a distance was a sweet and fragrant place, but close up, it had its hazards. Here, for instance, on a tree at the edge of the woods, readable in the moonlight, there was a notice: 'Beware of the Wodwo'.

It sounded like a crossword clue. Beware of the Wodwo. (4,3,2,3,5)

'Wodwo?' he asked tentatively.

'Wild Man of the Woods,' replied Miranda, and added, rather disdainfully, 'Do not be afeard. The Wodwo sleeps by night.' And then, almost with malice, 'But beware of Worms. They sally forth in darkness.'

Worms? Perhaps she had a thing about them, as some girls had about mice. He hoped they might meet one, so that he could show how brave he was. They had gone only a short way into the wood when he realized how confusing the Sudonian vocabulary could be. A huge snake hung from the branch of a tree and hissed in their faces.

'Harrow! A worm!' cried Miranda, and shrank back.

Sudonian snakes, or worms, are very unsociable, as they have two heads, and are thus able to answer themselves back. This one swayed before Jonah, the four pinpoints of its eyes glittering wickedly, with the obvious intention of hypnotizing him before swallowing him and then sleeping for six weeks. But Jonah was not lacking in courage, and being an engineer he always carried useful gadgets about him. He used one to good effect now. He whipped out his ballpoint pen, which had a tiny electric bulb in one end, and flashed it in the worm's eyes, moving it slowly back and forth. The worm's two heads began to turn inwards till they touched foreheads, and then outwards till it was looking left and right simultaneously. Pretty soon it decided that it was being hypnotized, rather than doing the hypnotizing, and with its two heads protesting peevishly to each other about Jonah's lack of sportsmanship, it flopped in coils on to the ground like Miss Wingbone's Long Thing, and slithered off into the undergrowth.

'Lo!' exclaimed Miranda, thrilled, 'there were a deed of derring-do, in sooth!'

'Oh, just a bit of good luck,' said Jonah modestly. But she transferred her crown to the hand farther from him, and took his hand in hers. With their fingers interlaced, they went on to Mad Waldo's hut.

Jonah found this delightful, but he was soon to learn again that Sudonia was full of surprises. Just as they reached the hut, and were about to knock on the door, three men in chain-mail strode out from behind the trees. They dispelled at once the myth that mediaeval men were only four feet high. The one in the middle was about three inches taller than the lanky Jonah, and much broader, while the other two were slightly smaller than elephants.

'False Sir Topas!' gasped Miranda.

'Come, my dear,' said the man in the middle, with a leer, 'you are surely most unwise to walk in this dangerous forest in the dead of night? You must let me and my men take care of you. Our horses are near at hand. Come.'

'Whither would you take me, sir?' asked Miranda, pale to the lips.

'For safety, to my own castle,' said Sir Topas, and

added informatively, 'Its walls are fourteen feet thick, and its spacious moat (recently restored) is full of man-eating fish. You will be protected there.'

'I do not need your protection, sir.'

'By your leave, maiden, you do.' He eyed Miranda and Jonah, who, struck with dismay, were still inter-laced. 'Why, even this worthy churl sees the need for it, and has so far forgot his station as to escort you.' He nodded briefly to his enormous followers, who, after bowing low, plucked Miranda from Jonah and held her deferentially but very firmly by each elbow, so that her feet hung slightly above the ground. Sir Topas took her crown and placed it carefully on her head. He turned to Jonah, still speaking with the same sardonic courtesy.

'Thank you for your service to my betrothed, well-meaning oaf. Be sure I shall remember it.'

He stretched out a chain-mail-gloved hand, seem-ingly to give Jonah a condescending pat on the shoulder, but really to give him a hard push, which sent him crashing down against the door of Mad Waldo's hut, where he lay momentarily stunned. Miranda gave a little squeak, but before she could utter another sound Sir Topas, saying, 'The night air is harmful to delicately nurtured damsels,' wound a scarf round and round her mouth and nose, and thus she was carried away, her toes brushing the earth, and her eyes rolling in despair.

CHAPTER FOUR

A light went on in the hut, the door opened, and two hands took Jonah under the armpits and dragged him inside.

'Strange garb,' a voice said. 'I would say clothes, but garb soundeth more historical.'

Jonah, recovering consciousness, recalled what had happened. He was aghast. Indeed, only those who have been torn from the side of a beautiful princess and flung against the hut of a mad magician at midnight can understand how he felt. He staggered to his feet.

'The princess,' he panted. 'She has been kidnapped. We must do something. We must not,' he added, with rising hysteria, for Mad Waldo seemed unperturbed, 'just stand here. We must act. Now.'

'Calmeth down,' said Mad Waldo, 'or should it be calm downeth? By my halidom, you must be the princess's great captain or chief from distant lands. Beshrew me, you're a rum choice. Verily, methought they had sent us the court clown.'

Jonah became exceedingly angry. 'Will you please get it into your head that we've got to do something, urgently?' he snapped. 'And another thing. Will you please not speak to me in Prithee English? I find such terms as "by my halidom", "beshrew me", "verily", and "methought", very irritating.'

'Yes, all right,' said Mad Waldo, with surprising mildness. 'I can't say I care for them myself. Being centuries ahead of my time, I ought long to have outgrown them. But as to rescuing the princess, you know, how do you expect to go about it? Rush out into the night after them? If you caught them, what would you do then? We must be more subtle than that.'

Jonah had used the very same words to the princess only a little while ago, and he saw the sense of them. He took stock of the mad magician. Waldo was built similarly to Jonah himself, being tallish and bony, but his eyes were a wild blue, and what looked like a thatch of straw on his head was in reality hair. He wore a monk's habit.

Jonah now looked round the hut. It was brightly lit: astonishingly, by electricity. The lighting was concealed, and so cunningly placed that it lit up everything without casting shadows. On every side, mirrors gleamed, so that Jonah saw himself full face and side face simultaneously, as in the photographs in police records. Benches were fitted all round the walls, littered with an agglomeration of what seemed to be scientific apparatus, in which wires and glass predominated. In the centre of the rush-covered floor was a small table bearing a curious device like an ice-cream cone, which slowly revolved, so that its stripes continually disappeared into its pointed tip in a compelling and tantalizing fashion.

'You have discovered electricity,' he remarked, 'but how on earth do you generate it here?'

'What you see,' said Mad Waldo, smiling indulgently, 'is a streak of lightning trapped. It goeth – sorry, *goes* – round and round this hut for ever, seeking outlet *here* – ' he indicated the revolving cone – ' but being returned continually to its source.'

28

'So you have invented perpetual motion,' said Jonah.

'You are an intelligent fellow,' said Mad Waldo. 'A pity you put up such a poor show just now. Our dames don't rate intelligence very highly.'

'Give me a chance, will you,' said Jonah crossly. 'I've only just got here.'

'But you were prepared for this visit, weren't you?'

'Prepared, nothing. I just happened to make a silly contraption for a dram. soc., and – ' Mad Waldo looked excusably puzzled. 'Look. Or for that matter, herkneth. Let me explain.'

He sat down on a bench and did so, the many images of himself mouthing and gesticulating in the mirrors. Mad Waldo listened, his expression, as the tale unrolled, moving from approval to rapture.

'Dear friend!' he exclaimed, when Jonah had finished. He took Jonah's hand in both his own and shook it warmly. 'Dear Oppo!'

'What?'

'Yes, of course. Too much to take in all at once. If I told you all, you could not stand it now. You must rest. And eat, perhaps? May I make you a mediaeval sandwich?'

'No thank you, but I am rather tired.'

'Of course. You shall rest. We will talk later. We shall talk to great effect.'

'The princess – ' said Jonah, distressed.

'Yes, yes. We shall rescue the pretty thing. Have no fear. We shall do that, and so much more. When you have rested, we shall talk, dear friend.' He began giggling wildly. 'Oh yes, we shall talk . . .'

After several days the engineers succeeded in remaking the frame of the mirror, and delivered the various parts to Miss Wingbone, who assembled them in her flat. This caused her little trouble, the mirror returning beautifully into position, as though suspended in space. She was unsure where to keep it. Reluctant to let it out of her sight, she took it to her office by day, and took it home again at night, making her arms ache in the process.

When she was doing this the second evening running, the junior clerk Peacock came upon her, and being a chivalrous youth, helped her carry it to the lift. At the bottom he helped her carry it to her car. As he happened to live not far from her (although in humbler circumstances), she drove him to her home where again he helped her carry the mirror into the lift, and then out of the lift into her flat. She made him a cup of tea.

'Is this Mr Sprockett's latest invention, Miss Wingbone?'

'That's right,' she replied, and unwrapped it from its sacking to show him. He was none the wiser when he saw it, of course, and yet it had an extraordinary effect on him. He sat gazing at it, as Sir Galahad might have done if he had accidentally bumped into the Holy Grail.

'You seem impressed, Peacock,' said Miss Wingbone, 'but do you know what it is?'

'Oh no, Miss Wingbone.' Peacock sounded slightly shocked, as if she had suggested something improper.

'Neither do I,' she said, and laughed. He looked at her in wonderment, and then back at the mirror. She looked at it too, and they were reflected in it side by side.

Miss Wingbone took off her spectacles and chewed her side-piece, a habit of hers. This of course turned her into a beautiful woman. Peacock saw her in the mirror. Their eyes met in reflection, and then he slowly turned and looked at her in the flesh. His lips were parted and his eyes were cloudy. It was plain that, on that sight, he had fallen hopelessly in love with her. He did not fall down in a swoon, to be sure, but he was certainly stunned with adoration, and might well have sat there for two years had she not gently taken his teacup from him and said, 'Well! I really must be getting on. Let me run you home.'

She drove the stricken youth home and came back frowning and biting her lip. She took off her spectacles and looked in Jonah's mirror. Good Heavens, she was a beautiful woman! Suspiciously, she consulted her own dressing-table mirror. She looked in this often enough, but only to comb her hair (which was golden and luxurious) and to apply a discreet amount of make-up; never properly to *look* at herself. She was amazed. Jonah's mirror had not flattered her. She was beautiful. She put her spectacles on again and sat awhile in thought. That poor boy! She shrugged her shoulders, but did not quite shrug off her agitation.

Well, this would never do. Now that she had the reconditioned mirror, she ought to use it somehow, but how? Up till now she had not dared to try working it, lest it should transport herself as it had done Jonah, possibly into a universe of some other parallel. She was reminded of the complaint of the Leeds manageress about the dishwasher. Suppose all Jonah's latest gadgets had this inborn fault, and the mirror flung people in all directions, as the dishwasher had done plates? She might land up in some parallel inhabited solely by dinosaurs. A fat lot of good that would do, wouldn't it? She spent the whole evening worrying, and went to bed without touching the mirror.

Like Jonah before her, she had a series of fragmentary dreams, but they were not like his, tantalizing glimpses of paradise. Each flash intimated, rather, that some deception was going on of which she was the victim. She would wake fitfully, then fall asleep again, and the dreams went on, tiresomely, as though the three-card trick were being repeatedly performed before her eyes, too slickly for her to spot the lady.

At last she woke up fully, and remembering what Jonah had told her, she went quietly and grimly into her living room, where the mirror stood. She drew the curtains and moved it so that the moonlight struck its face. It reflected an oblong of light on to the window. Miss Wingbone set her jaw. She now behaved childishly, as most of us are capable of doing when we are quite alone. She fetched a basinful of water and stood poised, determined that, if Jonah's dream valley manifested itself, and that girl happened to be in the offing, she would throw it all over her. And if Jonah happened to be with her, so much the better.

But no valley appeared, no door even. Vexed, she looked round at the mirror. A tiny spot of light showed just for a blink in its top lefthand corner. A few seconds later a succession of streaks crossed its face. Shakily, she turned the serrated wheel ever so little. A vertical line of white light split the mirror down the centre, as brilliant as a magnesium flare. She tried again. A blurred outline, roughly the shape of a man's head, came into sight. It might be Jonah! For that matter, it might be anyone: Moses, Genghis Khan. In agony to bring it into focus, she turned the wheel just a little more boldly, whereupon everything was lost. The mirror stood there blandly reflecting the moonlight, and no amount of swivelling it back and forth would get any more out of it.

'This co-director of yours,' said Mad Waldo, as they

partook of a breakfast tankard of mead, ' – intelligent, you say?'

'Arguably the cleverest woman in the world.'

'Is there any chance that she could reconstruct the mirror?'

'It's simple enough, but – '

'Let's pray that she does.'

'I can't wholeheartedly say amen to that,' said Jonah. 'I don't much want to go back. Sudonia has its dangers, like overgrown worms, false people, etc, but I could learn to live with them. A compulsion keeps me here.'

'Love,' said Waldo, and added gloomily, 'courtly, most likely.'

'Could be. Sooth to say, I am half dead for love of her.'

'Ah yes. That's it. And you would lose a world for love?'

'Quite honestly, it's not worth keeping,' said Jonah. 'I got very depressed inhabiting it.'

'But from what you've told me, it is a world of infinite opportunity. I should not be Mad Waldo there. I should be a giant, a marvel. Is there no hope that your fiancée might mend the mirror and try to get in touch with you?'

'It was probably destroyed by the lightning,' said Jonah uneasily.

'So there goes my only access to your world,' said Waldo bitterly. 'It is losing a genius.'

To call himself a genius was an understatement. He could recite his alphabet at the age of three months, and at six months was working out all the theorems of plane geometry with a stick in the dust. His parents, who were ignorant peasants, had never heard of plane geometry, and supposed that he was communicating with the devil. They had suspected him all along, as the Sudonians distrusted intellect, so they left him out in

33

the mountains to die. He was discovered by a passing magician (good) who took him home and raised him as his own son, and taught him all his magic lore. Very soon he surpassed his foster-father, and everyone else, and in his early teens was the greatest magician in the kingdom.

But of course he had developed on very different lines from Jonah, and in some ways he was staggeringly ignorant. He believed that his world was flat, and the centre of its universe, with the sun and stars revolving round it. He would not have even begun to understand the idea of a parallel universe. He believed simply that Jonah had come from 'a far distant land', a wonder-world out somewhere beyond the edge of his own.

On the other hand, he knew some things that were unknown in Jonah's world. Where the latter had gone the route of science, Waldo had gone the route of magic, and in some respects had gone much farther ahead. Supposing himself to be dealing with wizardry, he had achieved miracles of scientific invention, beside which the knubbing cleat and the sprockett hasp were as the early spinning wheel. Long before Jonah had blundered by sheer chance on Waldo's world, Waldo had been getting signals from Jonah's: voices, visions, fragmentary pictures. All he needed to establish contact properly was someone at the other end to receive him and respond. Then Jonah had made his mirror for the Ambleford Players, and contact was very nearly, but not quite, achieved.

At this point the Princess Miranda, unconvincingly disguised as a peasant girl, had come to Waldo for help. Her visit, he was sure, was more than a coincidence. Tremendously excited by the flickerings he was getting from Jonah's 'distant land' (they had begun when he used the mirror at the dram. soc.'s rehearsals) Waldo now became convinced that they were aimed at Miranda. She was royal, and a great prince out in the beyond was calling her. He had told her to kiss what he (using respectful capital letters) called The Cone, and she, the pretty creature, called 'the tiger-coloured stone', and await results.

The first encounter of Jonah and Miranda, frustrated though it was, thrilled Waldo beyond measure. Now that Jonah was here, and had described his world, Waldo was panting with eagerness to get into it. He was tired of Sudonia, tired of living in a hut in the woods and having to pick his way through worms and wodwos, tired of being called mad, and even tired of Miranda, who, though a pretty creature, was high-handed with mad magicians and took his aid for granted.

Jonah wakened him from his reverie.

'The princess – '

'You do harp on that subject,' said Waldo, 'but there, that's what you're here for. It is your destiny.'

'If I save her, what will happen to me?'

'The king will give you her hand in marriage.'

Jonah's head reeled with the vision of being married to that exquisite creature, and of perhaps ultimately becoming the Good King of a land where, all the bad people having been eliminated, everybody would be good. He had just the slightest qualm for Hubert; when he learned that Miranda had married, might it not kill him off altogether? But before he could mention this, or any of the dozen things that came into his head, Waldo gave a shout.

'The Cone!'

Indeed The Cone, which normally revolved in a clockwise direction, was swinging back and forth as though trying to rock itself out of its own monotony.

'By the Rood, there is contact!' cried Waldo, lapsing into the dialect in his delight. 'Behold!'

Begrudgingly, Jonah beheld; but as it turned out, there was not much to behold. There were a few squiggles of light, one vertical streak of great brilliance, and once, for the fraction of a second, the vaguest outline of a human head, hanging in mid-air. Then nothing. As though resignedly, The Cone resumed its normal course.

All the same, he knew what it meant. Miss Wingbone had put the mirror together again. He might have known she would. She was arguably the cleverest woman in the world.

CHAPTER FIVE

Miss Wingbone stopped the supply of newspapers and milk for Jonah's flat, and let it be known that he was away on business, but she knew that in time people would grow suspicious. The rumour might even spread that she had murdered him. Her own neighbours were already casting curious glances at the wrapped-up object that she was carting in and out every day. Perhaps they thought it was Jonah's remains. A little thought would tell them that parcels of Jonah's remains would not always be the same shape and size, nor would she, having removed them from her flat in the morning, take equal care to bring them back at night; but rumour and reason do not go readily together.

Life at work was no less worrying. A firm called Towpath Ltd was making a takeover bid for Sprockett's Electricals, and kept sending out letters to shareholders urging them to change sides. Miss Wingbone fought this by also sending letters to shareholders insisting that Towpath Ltd were bankrupt scoundrels, and imploring them to stay put, and for extra safety to buy more shares in Sprockett's. The cost of this campaign was swallowing up the firm's money, and she longed for Jonah to come back, if only to give her moral support.

Peacock was worrying her too. For herself, she had always dismissed love as sentimental folly, but she knew that other young people were not as strong as she was, and was very patient with them. Indeed, if she'd been so inclined, she would have made an excellent agony aunt. Peacock's enslavement touched her, all the more because he said nothing, but simply pined away. She gave him a piece of cake to eat with his morning tea. He wrapped it up and took it home, to keep as a sacred relic, she supposed. As far as she could tell, he had stopped eating altogether.

She tried to protect him from the full glare of herself, as it were, by taking to dark glasses, enormous replicas of her normal pair, which she sometimes wore on holiday. They gave her a goddesslike air of mystery which succeeded only in making Peacock feel more hopeless than ever. His work for the story-writing course fell behind.

In face of all this, there seemed to be only one thing she could do: get Jonah back, somehow, from wherever he was, and, to keep him out of further mischief, marry him.

In spite of all the evidence so far, she still doubted the idea that he had slipped into a parallel universe; and so, she reflected grimly, would the police. Yet those squiggles and flickers of light must have meant something, surely? The next evening, having cooked herself a brand of frozen food of which the TV advertisements spoke very highly, but which in fact tasted like damp plasticine, she set about working the mirror this way and that.

While doing so, she kept being reminded of Peacock. It was as if the mirror itself were bringing him to mind; as if it could throw up references to him, as it could throw out flecks of light. Once again, but more strongly this time, she sensed some connection between his hang-ups and what had happened to Jonah. But what?

She shook her head. She distrusted intuition, feminine or otherwise. There was no reason for feeling like this. Frowning, she concentrated on the job in hand. But this time she got no response whatever, not even a squiggle, and after a while she packed it in and did the washing up.

Bevis, the king of Sudonia, paced distractedly through his palace. His steps made hollow echoes in the great chambers, as most of the furniture was missing, having been used to pay gambling debts.

Being a good king, he was upset over the disappearance of his daughter Miranda. The Lord Chamberlain had told him a disturbing tale. Late the previous night, a serving wench had observed a young woman in peasant dress, but with a crown on her head, slinking from the palace grounds in the direction of the hills. It might be, she thought, a peasant girl up to some rustic buffoonery, or it might be the princess herself going to a fancy dress ball.

'Wretched girl, why did she not stop her?'

'She was in a difficult position, Sire,' remonstrated the Lord Chamberlain. 'As a palace employee, it was beneath her dignity to speak to a peasant, and as a servant it would have been presumptuous to speak to the princess.'

'Bah.'

'Yes, Sire.'

'In the night, too,' said the king gloomily. 'Perchance has she by now been swallowed by a worm.'

Worm catches early bird, thought the Lord Chamberlain, who was quite a wit, but lacked an outlet for his talent. He looked searchingly out of the window, as if the mere outdoors might suggest a course of action, and saw two figures approaching the palace. They halted at the edge of the moat. One looked like Mad Waldo, except that he had shoulder-length black hair and wore not a monk's habit, but a flowered tunic of shrieking loudness. The other, equally tall and skinny, wore a suit of black velvet, and a decorated sword at his side.

'Whatever they have come for, it is too late,' said the king, following his gaze. 'Miranda is lost. So are we all. Lost, lost.' And he sank to the floor, there being no chair to arrest his progress.

He did, however, suffer the travellers to enter, after someone had been found to work the drawbridge, for the palace was short of staff as well as furniture. He ascended his throne, which he had managed to hang on to, and the two men knelt before him. The flowery one brought alarming news. Miranda was held prisoner by a false knight who had carried her off under cover of darkness.

'Wherefore wotst thou this?' asked the king, proving that at least he hadn't lost his diction, for this is not easy to say.

The flowery one drew breath and began:

'Creeping at midnight through the perilous wood –' but the king cut in, hastily.

'No blank verse, please. It takes so long to get to the point. Deliver a plain, unvarnished tale.'

The flowery one did so. His black-suited companion was a great captain or chief from far-off lands, and he himself was his squire. Taking a short cut through the woods by night, on their way to the palace, they had espied a trio of false knights carrying off a damsel, who from her royal bearing and the fact that she was swinging a crown by her side, they took to be the princess of this gracious land.

'We would have intervened, vanquished them, and

rescued the maiden,' said the flowery one, 'but we are strangers here, and could not risk violating knightly etiquette.'

'You'd have been wasting your time,' said the king. 'From your description, that was False Sir Topas and his crew. You are right about their being false, but they have a claim to her.' And he explained Miranda's predicament.

'In that case, Sire,' said the flowery one, who did not seem surprised, 'you must stake all on a gamble.'

The Lord Chamberlain gave a hollow groan, but the king's eyes glinted at the temptation of his fatal addiction.

'What sort of a gamble?'

'Your palace and your kingdom against the release of your daughter and the cancellation of all your debts.'

The Lord Chamberlain gave a cry of horror, but the king asked, 'And what shall be the nature of the wager?'

'My master here shall defeat False Sir Topas in single combat.'

The king's jaw dropped.

'*Him*?'

'The same.'

'He does not look as if he could bear the weight of a suit of armour.'

'My master despises armour. He will fight him as he is dressed now.'

'With what weapons?'

'With his trusty sword.'

The king eyed the decorative piece by the black-suited one's side. It looked fitter for slitting open billets-doux than for fighting.

'Do not hesitate, your Majesty. This is a dead cert.'

The Lord Chamberlain, who was groaning on the

floor, managed to splutter, 'We've heard that one before,' but the words 'dead cert' never failed to seduce the king.

'He has magic powers, perhaps? Some secret up his sleeve?'

'Indeed he has, Sire. Up both sleeves.'

'We didn't tell him the exact truth,' said Jonah.

'That's all right, because we're good,' said Waldo, and took off his black wig and flowered coat.

'Are you sure this Sir Topas will honour the bet if he loses?'

'He'll have to. He'd never live it down in Sudonia if he didn't.'

'Are you sure this sword is all that trusty?'

'With our combined genius behind it? Of course.'

'I hope it is,' said Jonah. 'The only sword-fighting I've ever done was with my father, with a little wooden sword when I was about five.'

'You must have faith. You must believe in yourself.'

'You sound like my psychiatrist,' said Jonah gloomily.

'He sounds a worthy fellow. And now, if you are agreeable, we'll try again to contact your fiancée.'

'Must we? Can't we leave it till after the fight?'

'No time like the present,' said Waldo, sounding this time like Miss Wingbone; and he began positioning the mirrors that lined his walls, determined not to be caught napping as he had been before.

It was Saturday afternoon in Sudonia, and also in our own world, for the two, although some centuries apart in culture, and at variance in their seasons, synchron-ized in hours of the day. Miss Wingbone had just finished another dreadful meal of frozen food and was worrying about Peacock, who had beyond doubt eaten nothing for his lunch. Yesterday morning she had given him a slab of chocolate. By the afternoon he had bought a little perspex box to keep it in, tied round with a bow of gold braid.

Thinking about Peacock led her to thinking about Jonah, her other protégé. However would he look after himself in another universe, for Heaven's sake, without even a change of socks? He was helpless enough even in another town.

Perhaps that girl would show him around . . .

Miss Wingbone's face darkened and her pulse quickened. To become agitated like this impaired the reasoning of her excellent brain. She controlled herself, and her brain had an innings of its own. *What* girl? Show him around *where*?

Once again, the doubts she had never shaken off completely came flooding back. Jonah had been in a pretty shaky state recently, visiting psychiatrists, lusting after traffic wardens, etc. Could he possibly have imagined himself into disappearing? Was she most childishly letting herself be drawn into it?

She sat huddled up in her kitchen, thinking hard on these lines, telling herself that she really must stop believing in fantasies and begin a proper search for him. Then, like one who, having convinced herself that she must give up smoking, slinks to a drawer and opens a fresh packet of cigarettes, she went hesitantly into her living room, drew the curtains, and began turning the serrated wheel on the mirror.

At the same time, in the heart of the worm-infested, wodwo-ridden wood in Sudonia, Mad Waldo was tuning all his instruments to make contact with her. And so contact was established. Miss Wingbone's curtains became a frame of solid black in which three thin lines of light outlined a door. As she crept towards it the door slowly opened. When at last she stood in the doorway, she found herself staring not at the pretty scene that Jonah had described, but at trees, so numerous that she couldn't see the wood for them. A snake with two heads reared up, took one look at her, and slithered off. A wild-looking man in skins peered round a tree, then disappeared with a panic-stricken yell. She was still wearing her dark glasses, which had naturally frightened these simple creatures, but she did not realize this, and was rather offended.

The scene tilted, so that for a moment she was looking over the very tops of the trees, and then, as it righted itself, she felt as if she were being rushed noiselessly forward, the trees skimming past her to left and right. Alarmed, she stared round, sure that she had been precipitated right out of her own world into this alien wood; but no, she was still in the doorway, and the objects in her living room were still solid behind her. The trees, not herself, were moving. They were reeling up and slipping past as if on a screen. Some sort of cabin loomed up, till it stood so near that its frontage filled her vision.

And then, as if she were looking at a stage in the theatre, she could see the inside. At first all that struck her was a battery of mirrors, winking and gleaming with light thrown out by a revolving cone-shaped object in the centre. Then she saw the two men. One was a straw-haired bony fellow crouching behind the cone, squinting and pulling extraordinary faces. The other, in a black velvet suit with a cream collar and cuffs, and rather more fully bearded than when she had seen him last, was Jonah.

CHAPTER SIX

She was very close to him. One step, and she would be inside the hut. And yet she was not. When she tried to enter it, it eluded her. She could get no farther. She veered round, and found herself looking at the wall of her own living room. She tacked off, and found herself looking at the wall opposite. Nothing she could do would move her forward. She stood framed in the doorway.

She saw that the straw-haired fellow was making equal efforts to contact her. He stretched out his arm, groping blindly. It was as if he were trying to reach her through glass.

He stopped trying, crawled under a bench and began fiddling with some wires. Jonah's mouth, meanwhile, was opening and shutting with no sound coming from it. After a while speech of a sort became audible, but as if a disc were being played at too high a speed: a chipmunk delivery. The straw-haired one made an adjustment and Jonah's speech came out in a slurred and heavy drawl. Another adjustment, and his speech became sharp and clear.

'Ah, that's better. Mad Waldo. Miss Wingbone.'

'How do you do,' said Miss Wingbone perfunctorily. 'Jonah – '

'Welcome to Sudonia, Miss Wingbone,' said Waldo.

She ignored him. 'Jonah,' she said impatiently, 'change out of that silly suit and come home.'

'Can't,' said Jonah pertly, like some small boy. Which was true enough. But Miss Wingbone did not feel reasonable.

'You are being totally irresponsible. Do you know how much business is getting lost while you're gallivanting about here?' Her pent-up emotions were loosing themselves in a torrent and although she felt the need to check them she could not. 'Do you know that other firms are making takeover bids? Do you know – '

Jonah now did what he always did in these confrontations. He fished in the pocket of the velvet suit and pulled out a crumpled page from *The Times*.

'Paint the natives with angry words, eight letters?'

Normally, Miss Wingbone would solve the clue at once and sweep the interruption aside. She made to do so now, but for the first time in her life she could not. Perhaps stress was distracting her mind.

'Er . . .' she faltered; then, furiously: 'Jonah, surely we shouldn't discuss *The Times* crossword at this juncture?'

'You don't think it could be a proverb, do you, like paint the lily, sort of thing?'

'No I do not,' snapped Miss Wingbone 'Anyway, paint the lily's not a proverb, it's Shakespeare.'

'But Shakespeare's proverbial. You could say, a proverb of Shakespeare's.'

'You could not.'

'Yes you could.'

'Well, if you did, you'd be a fool.'

'I have lost track of this conversation,' said Mad Waldo mildly, 'but, dear Miss Wingbone, will you please not stamp your foot like that? The least vibration may throw the mirror out of focus.'

Miss Wingbone saw the point and from now on hardly dared to breathe.

'I could offer you a flagon of mead,' said Waldo sociably, 'but there seems to be a barrier between us.'

'I got here by lightning,' said Jonah. 'It needs another storm. And even if there were one, of course, there's no guarantee – '

'Do you mean to say,' said Miss Wingbone, 'that we are restricted to just staring at one another?'

'For the time being, yes,' said Waldo. 'It's better for you than for us. We can see one scene only: yourself, and the weak outlines of your tastefully furnished room. You will be able to watch Jonah wherever he goes.'

'But can I – ' exploded Miss Wingbone, then remembered vibrations and said in a tense whisper: 'Can I never bring him back to earth?'

'For the time being, no,' said Waldo. 'Unless we can devise something, we shall have to wait till he is again struck by lightning, which, of course, could be dangerous. It could mean that all you got back to earth would be a smoking heap of bones.'

'You're mad,' said Miss Wingbone in a vibrant undertone.

'So they say,' said Waldo affably.

'Look on the bright side,' said Jonah, who now seemed to have recovered his spirits. 'It'll be like watching TV. Besides, even if you got here, you might not like it, you know. They say the grass is always greener on the other side.'

'The grass isn't in the *least* greener,' said Miss Wingbone, impatience turning her cautious whisper to a hiss. 'With all due respect to your host, I can only describe your situation as *barbaric*. I have *no intention* of trying to visit this – this – '

47

'Sudonia,' said Waldo, 'and barbaric is right, Miss Wingbone. My dearest wish is to leave it and join your world.'

'You're an inventor, aren't you?' said Miss Wingbone to Jonah. 'What are you going to do about it?'

Jonah consulted the crossword again.

'Do you think it might be "warpaint"? Warpaint is eight letters.'

'Of course it couldn't.'

'All right, then,' said Jonah, nettled, 'you think of something better.'

'I have no intention of doing so.'

'I'm going to put warpaint.'

'Don't be *absurd*. You'll mess the whole puzzle up.'

'I don't care.'

'Well, if you want to make a fool of yourself – '

'Please,' protested Waldo.

Miss Wingbone drew a deep breath, then, carefully avoiding the mirror which still stood there, emitting significant flashes, she withdrew to the other side of her living room and sank on to the sofa, from where she was lost in shadows to the men in the hut.

'I simply do not believe this,' she said. 'I am not dreaming, I am not drunk, I am not insane, it is happening in daylight, it is real, but I do not believe it. It strains credulity too far. I do not believe it.'

And despite the fact that the door was still open in the black wall opposite her, despite the fact that she could hear Jonah and Waldo calling her and that she had only to cross the room to see them again, she still refused to accept it. She was not alone in her obstinacy. Most of us share it with her. The truth is often too much for us. We believe only what's plausible.

For a moment, irrelevantly, she thought of Peacock. Something she had said to him, something he had

48

done? Some connection between him and Jonah? What *was* it . . . ? Then she frowned and cleared her mind of him, and threaded her way back to the magic door.

Calmer now, they came to an agreement. She could, as Jonah had suggested, use her mirror like a TV set. Jonah told her how to fix its position to keep it in focus by using a clothes peg. (Like many great inventions, his could be operated by the humblest means.) Waldo would 'transmit' to her as often as he thought prudent, by arranging his own set of mirrors appropriately.

'It's the best we can do for the present,' said Jonah, who was in better spirits than was seemly.

'It'll pass the winter evenings, I suppose,' said Miss Wingbone. She was not at all in good spirits. She covered the mirror with a large plastic bag and stood it carefully in a corner.

The whole of Sudonia was in a state of big fight fever. Not for years had a contest generated so much excitement as the forthcoming one between Jonah and False Sir Topas. This was partly because the folk were somewhat deprived of sporting events. Now and then a knight would ride in bearing the head of a dragon, but such trophies were always kept from close inspection, and the suspicion ran that they were fakes, concocted by magicians for a fee, for the purpose of enhancing the bearers in the eyes of Princess Miranda, whose hand every young man of breeding craved. Since False Sir Topas had won Miranda in a wager, such feats had ceased.

Another reason for the excitement was Jonah himself. He was such an improbable match for the great Sir

Topas that the rumour arose that there must be more to him than met the eye. Deep in the mythology of Sudonia there was a legend that a slender shepherd lad had once defeated an armoured giant with a stone from a sling, and the Sudonians, who were on the whole touchingly optimistic, began telling each other that this incident was going to be repeated.

Yet another reason, strongest in the palace itself, was Jonah's confidence. If he had shown any doubts at first, he concealed them now. He did no training and refused the aid of sparring partners. When warned of the invincible might of Sir Topas, he laughed, and if anyone persisted, he fell about.

There were two causes of this. One was that, in the course of a tough business life, with scoundrelly rivals like Towpath Ltd always in the offing, Jonah had learned the value of bluff. Always behave as though victory were certain. Never show doubt. The other was faith in his sword. Not for nothing had the genius of two worlds been put into the making of that weapon.

So great was Jonah's confidence that the wind of it even began to worry False Sir Topas's own backers. When a herald rode up to the latter's castle, blew a tucket, and called the terms of Jonah's challenge in tones that rang across the moat, they warned their champion to be wary.

'Belike skulduggery breweth, Sire,' one of them counselled. ' 'Tis e'en conceivable that yon varlet in velvet hath dealings with witches, and seeketh to vanquish you by means of the black art.'

''Tis e'en like,' echoed another. 'Morpeth, here, had a sweven to that effect.'

'A what?' said Sir Topas, who was rather ill-read.

'A sweven, or dream.'

'Ha!' said Sir Topas. 'Well, I am *not* such stuff as

dreams are made on. Let him pit his art against this!' He tossed a silk kerchief into the air, and, as it wafted down, drew his sword and with a swift stroke cut it in two. Everyone applauded, but doubts were not wholly dispelled. 'Mayhap,' muttered Sir Topas's supporters to one another, 'yon velvet-clad will be less amenable than a silk kerchief.' And behind his back, they hedged their bets by laying money on Jonah.

Eftsoons the level sward in the grounds of the king's palace was fully prepared for the combat, but not eftsoons enough for Miss Wingbone, who, while preparations were going on, had been kept totally in the dark. Every evening she would position the mirror and wait in vain for contact. She even took to nipping home at lunch-times, with the same lack of result. For all her strength of mind, she began to wear a lost look, as though her thoughts were far away, as indeed they were, as far away as human thought could be, although it is also true that, in a manner of speaking, they were on her own doorstep. Peacock, noticing her demeanour, began to tremble with hope and dread, so that the pounding of his heart made the out-tray on his desk rattle. The in-tray was weighed down with neglected correspondence.

But Miss Wingbone, in her anxiety, forgot about Peacock and didn't bring him any more cakes or slabs of chocolate. She missed Jonah and needed him. She was not inventive, and his inventiveness not only kept Sprockett's Electricals moving, but supplied a force which was lacking in her own life. She wondered if she would ever solve any more crossword clues for him. In Waldo's hut, he had shown a relief to be separated from her that bordered on hilarity, and she began to believe, with dismay, that he intended to stay that way.

She was thrilled, therefore, when one Saturday

afternoon she got through to Sudonia again. Standing in the impassable doorway, she found herself looking out on a wide green field, round which a great throng of people were seated in tiers. Her eye took in rank upon rank of knights in well-cut surcoats, young squires in flowered blouses as fresh as the month of May, and ladies, all looking alike in pointed hats. What did she see next but Jonah himself, still wearing the black velvet suit, sauntering to the centre of the field amid a great buzz of expectation from the spectators.

'Jonah!' she called sharply, like a mother to a child who is playing in the mud. 'What are you up to?'

But it was plain that he could neither see nor hear her. Her voice, her figure in the doorway, it seemed, were transmitted to Waldo's hut alone. Waldo had already told her as much.

Having reached the centre, Jonah turned and bowed, his back being to Miss Wingbone. The bow was directed at a young girl, distinguishable from the other dames by the crown on her head. Miss Wingbone saw, even at that distance, that her beauty was literally out of this world. Her golden hair streamed over her shoulders and hung in ripples over her bosom. Her blue, blue eyes sparkled more brilliantly than the jewels in her crown. She smiled, and her teeth were pearls. Miss Wingbone felt quite faint with dismay.

Miranda was seated, as befitted her ambiguous position, exactly between the king's followers and the supporters of False Sir Topas. Both sides were about equal in number, the king's followers wearing white to show that they were good, and those of Sir Topas also wearing white, falsely. King Bevis sat to the right of his daughter, nervously biting his nails. On his other side sat the Lord Chamberlain, looking glumly resigned, for he was a sceptic. A dreadful-looking henchman of Sir

Topas sat on Miranda's left, and eyed her like a guard dog.

'What *has* he let himself in for?' muttered Miss Wingbone.

A huge man, clanking in chain-mail from head to foot, strode on to the field bearing a shield that covered him from chin to knee, and waving a mighty sword. A long 'A-a-ah!' rose from the crowd, and some hisses, which the knight acknowledged, bowing ironically. Miss Wingbone could not bear to look. She hardly heard the words of the announcer, though they rang through the field: ' . . . The man ye love to hate: False Sir Topas! . . . AND, from far-off lands, introducing to you: ye mystery knight, Jonah of the Sprockett Hasp!' Covering her face with her hands, she backed away and almost collided with the mirror, and when she forced herself to look again, the fight was on.

Sir Topas advanced, brimming with confidence, his shield hung carelessly loose, and his sword poised to strike like a snake at Jonah's first move. Jonah crossed one leg in front of the other and leaned on his slender sword like an umbrella. Sir Topas hesitated for an instant, but, veteran of a hundred battles, he was used to surprise tactics, and his response was expert and deadly. Or at least, it ought to have been deadly. He jabbed like lightning at the sword on which Jonah was nonchalantly leaning, intending as Jonah lost balance to fetch him a back-hand swipe that would finish the contest. But this man, who could cut a fly in half as it flew, incredibly missed his aim, and missed it so badly that he stumbled and fell, sounding like a cascade of tin kettles. Jonah looked at him with scientific interest, moved back, and waited for him to regain his feet.

Sir Topas charged in now, stabbing and slashing; but each stab and each slash seemed weirdly misdirected.

He missed his aim again and again, and grew red in the face and began to breathe hard. Jonah held his sword like a taper, merely moving it searchingly about in front of him, and making no attempt to strike back. He didn't need to; Sir Topas was running himself into the ground. He not only missed, he followed through with his whole body, so that he staggered and fell over his own feet, or got his shield between his legs, and fell headlong time after time.

'Phew!' said Miss Wingbone. She understood. She knew the principle behind the bossle wheel, the knubbing cleat and the sprockett hasp, and indeed the mirror itself: magnetism. Jonah's genius had taught him how to use magnetism two ways: to attract in the normal way, but also, when needed, to repel. Possibly something like that had got into the dishwasher that upset the manageress in Leeds. The fact was that, as long as Sir Topas used a metal sword, he had no chance, for every blow would be spun aside by Jonah's negative-magnetic one, and the harder the blow the more violent its diversion.

Miss Wingbone's satisfaction was short-lived. She saw that the glamorous creature in the crown, opposite, was bouncing up and down and clapping her hands and laughing with glee, and she could tell what Jonah's reward would be when he had won. She even felt indignant: he was not fighting fair! It was like a boxer slipping a horseshoe into his glove!

But then, what would be 'fair'? To fight Sir Topas with his own weapons and let him use all his tremendous advantages?

She recalled that all was said to be fair in love and war.

Love as well, she thought, miserably.

The Sudonian onlookers, however, had no mixed

feelings. They fell out of their seats laughing; they clung to one another, the tears of merriment pouring down their faces. Even the supporters of Sir Topas joined in. Laughter rocked the field. Laughter is a universal language, and seldom kind.

It maddened Sir Topas and spurred him to a final effort. Casting aside his shield, he held his sword aloft with both hands and charged. Jonah, in response, drew his own sword daintily through the air in the manner of a pastrycook drawing a thin line on a cake, and then cut a quick circle with it. The sword of Sir Topas spun from his hand, turned over several times in air, and fell point downwards into the sward a dozen paces away. Sir Topas stumbled, floundered, and fell to his knees, from which position he sat back on his heels and gazed up at Jonah pathetically.

Everyone in the crowd stood up.

'Hew him jauntilie, withal!'

'Hack him manfullie!'

But instead of administering the *coup de grâce*, Jonah beckoned, and a thin dark-haired man, whom Miss Wingbone spotted immediately as Mad Waldo in a black wig, crossed the sward to confer with him. After they had exchanged a few words, the dark-haired one went over to the announcer, who strode forward and proclaimed:

'Jonah of the Sprockett Hasp declineth to strike an unarmed man! Let False Sir Topas recover his sword and continue, an he will, or else e'en concede victory for the nones!'

Sir Topas remained sitting on his heels, too exhausted to move. Brokenly he shook his head, in defeat.

Thundering cheers, many of them coming from the ranks of Sir Topas's own supporters, who, having secretly backed Jonah at long odds, were well pleased with the result. King Bevis, beaming, as well he might, for he had verily hit the jackpot, began leading his radiant daughter across the grass to congratulate the winner.

But hold. There is an ugly reaction in a section of the crowd. Some twenty or so of Sir Topas's followers, the most beef-witted of them, who have not had the fore-sight to hedge their bets, have stormed on to the pitch, bellowing their dissent.

'Witchcraft!'

''Tis haply a frame-up, forsooth!'

The king shrank back, protecting his daughter; the few who had followed him scattered; and the twenty false knights, waving battle-axes and spiked metal balls on chains, lumbered across the field to Jonah and sur-rounded him.

Jonah held his sword at arm's length and spun rapidly round and round, as one may see a skater do on ice. After a number of spins he reversed and spun in the opposite direction, no doubt to counteract giddiness. The result was devastating. His twenty-odd assailants were flung about like leaves in a whirlwind, and hurtled into one another with a clashing and scraping of metal to set the teeth on edge. Jonah's only danger was from the weapons that flew through the air. But these, by good fortune, crashed back among their owners, to their even greater discomfort; and in a short while the scene looked like a demolition yard.

And now the crowd went absolutely insane with excitement, for never in their history had there been a feat to equal this. Jonah, feeling forward with his sword like a water-diviner, picked his way through his fallen attackers, who, as the sword came near to them, were rolled violently aside. One by one they picked them-selves up and limped off the field, certainly sadder, but probably not wiser, for they were a bone-headed lot. And so Jonah came face to face with King Bevis and the Princess Miranda.

'Noble sir,' quoth she, for she was given to quothing at times of high drama, 'verily hast thou worshipfully won worship!'

Jonah replied modestly that it was all a bit of jolly good luck, actually.

Everyone at this point had forgotten False Sir Topas, who was still sitting on his heels, all in. The Princess Miranda now made a gracious gesture. She went over to him, bade him rise, and handed him a single rose.

It wasn't clear where she had got a single rose from at such short notice, and she must have supposed that Sir Topas could be easily satisfied; but anyway, he affixed it to his helm and walked with bowed shoulders away. And now the crowd, who in turn had got hold of masses of flowers from somewhere, festooned Jonah and Miranda with them, and the two of them were led off amidst scenes of the wildest joy to the palace in the background, from where, in a short while, they reappeared on the balcony, wreathed with flowers, the king between them, wreathed in smiles, and the crowds below them pouring forth a thundering storm of love.

This scene, from Miss Wingbone's point of view, was far off and rather out of focus, as if she were looking through the small end of an ill-adjusted telescope. After a while the trio left the balcony and the crowd dispersed, leaving her only the empty, littered field to stare at. This would be her only view, she supposed, till Waldo got back to his hut and retuned his apparatus. Some birds settled on the field and began pecking. They depressed her exceedingly. She covered the mirror up and went despondently to her kitchen to cook another awful meal of frozen food.

But she stopped and looked back to where her curtains, her perfectly normal curtains, hung about her perfectly normal windows.

'I do not believe it,' she said aloud. 'I simply do *not* believe it.'

CHAPTER SEVEN

Again and again Miss Wingbone told herself, 'I must believe it, because it is real.' She felt as a psychiatrist must feel, forced to take seriously the hang-ups of his patients. She even went so far as to ring up Jonah's own psychiatrist, hoping to discuss it with him, but she found that he was on sick leave, having a nervous breakdown.

'But then,' she said, 'it is *not* all in the mind, is it? It's in the window end of my living room. It's absurd. But the fact remains.'

Why, she wondered, had she been allowed to witness Jonah's victory over False Sir Topas? Wasn't he all too eager to get shot of her? She soon learned that it had been Mad Waldo, not Jonah, who had been responsible for that bit of viewing.

Several times during the week after it, she had tried to make contact again. She failed each time, not without relief, for she dreaded coming upon Jonah in the embrace of that creature in the crown. When at last she did get in touch it was with Waldo, not Jonah. He now lived in a room in the palace, being accepted as Jonah's squire. Yes, very comfortable, thanks, except that the black wig made his head itchy. No, Jonah and Miranda were not married yet; things moved slowly and ceremonially in Sudonia. Nor were they embracing.

Courtship in Sudonia was strictly formal.

That was something, anyway.

With difficulty, by night, Waldo had gradually transferred all his gear from the hut in the woods to his handsome new room in the palace, and set it up there. Anticipating that his old hut would still be visited (he had done a brisk trade as a mad magician) he left an answering device, a voice which spoke out whenever there was a knock at the door:

'Mad Waldo is agone for the nones, but, an't please thee, thou mayst leave him word. Stateth first what thou'rt hight, and eke speaketh thy message, starting . . . *now*.'

The one or two visitors who heard this peeped through the hut window, puzzled, and when they saw that it was empty, ran off in terror.

'Waldo,' asked Miss Wingbone, who was now on friendly terms with him, like a pen-pal or a radio ham, 'why do Sudonians speak such a muddled-up language? It's part mediaeval, part bad Shakespearean, part modern and completely phoney.'

He could not explain this, but it was one of the few things he could not explain. His understanding was phenomenal. She estimated that his IQ must be about twelve hundred. He explained Sudonian life to her and made it radiantly clear. She soon had a grasp of all that had happened to Jonah. In turn, she described earthly life to him. She was beginning to like him so much that she gave him a friendly warning about entering our world.

'You'd be terribly disillusioned, Waldo. It's a mad house.'

'There's no future in Sudonia,' he replied sadly.

Since, however, there seemed no chance of either side's crossing to the other, there was not much point in discussing it.

Jonah, too, was finding life in Sudonia slow. The king had formally given him Miranda's hand in marriage, but 'formally' was the operative word. He might have known that in a world where a swoon could last two years, there would be no breakneck pace anywhere. He never met Miranda alone. She was always accompanied by at least twenty-four ladies, and they spent much of their time dancing in a ring, and, when they got tired of this, dancing round in the opposite direction. He was at a loose end most of the time. Now and then, from sheer loneliness, he went to Waldo's room and helped him with his experiments, until finally he interrupted him while he was speaking to Miss Wingbone. Embarrassed, he fished *The Times* crossword from his pocket.

'This one, "paint the natives with angry words",' he began, 'I was wondering – '

'Oh, we've done that,' said Waldo. 'Diatribe.'

'Dye-a-tribe, see?' said Miss Wingbone brightly. 'Waldo's awfully good at it, Jonah. He'd never seen a crossword in his life, and now he can solve all the clues in a puzzle simultaneously.'

'Marvellous,' said Jonah wanly.

'Just a bit of jolly good luck, actually,' said Waldo.

Miss Wingbone was plainly very taken with Waldo and it made Jonah slightly jealous. He tried to persuade himself that it was a good thing, it relieved him of an embarrassing commitment, and the best thing that could happen would be for Waldo to break through into Jonah's world and take Miss Wingbone off his hands, leaving himself to lifelong bliss here with Miranda. It ought to be bliss, oughtn't it? What, marry a princess of unearthly beauty and be in line to this land of perpetual summer as king? In spite of all this, he could not wholly convince himself. 'Twas not so sweet now as it was before.

To his dismay, he began to feel returning twinges of the depression that had started all this. His mood did not improve when he met Hubert, Miranda's lovesick admirer, who now lived about the court. Swooning seemed to be the only physical action he was capable of, but 'swoon' was a comparative term. Hubert had not lain in a coma for two years, as Jonah had imagined, but simply went about sighing and throwing himself full-length on couches, or (when in the open air) on daisied banks. He followed Miranda about, made sheep's eyes, and sang love songs in a plaintive tenor voice. He wrote the lyrics himself. They were full of alliteration and extra e's.

> Shee untoe mee suche crueltie doth shewe,
> Methinks she walloweth in her own disdaine;
> Wearie with wanhope doe I waile my woe,
> Being by her moste pitilesslie slaine,
> Or (at the leest) quite doubled up with paine . . .

He was clearly enjoying himself. Sometimes Miranda and her ladies, having danced both clockwise and anti-clockwise for a while, would pause and look senti-mentally at one another, after which Miranda would approach the youth and give him a single rose. She seemed to have a ready stock of single roses. Hubert, having carefully wrapped up the stem to avoid pricking himself, would clasp it to his heart and swoon again.

'Why do you encourage him?' asked Jonah impatiently.

'Surely, my lord, thou wouldst not have me slay him by my disregard?'

'Yes, I think I wouldst, and I think he wouldst, too, from the way he goes on about it.'

But the ladies all laid their heads on one side and looked reproachful.

62

'What does he hope to get out of it?' persisted Jonah.

'Alas, nothing, my lord. Forever must he protest his love, and forever must I virtuously deny him.'

'And it'll go on like that for ever?'

'Even so, my lord.'

'So that's the game, is it? Well, I feel like a first reserve.'

Jonah turned on his heel and strode off. Miranda said complacently to her ladies:

'Heedeth not. My lord hath a distemper.'

Jonah heard this and swung round. 'Can you wonder at it?' he demanded. 'It's a dog's life.'

He was soon sorry for what he had said. He was supposed to be Miranda's glamorous prince, and he was not playing the part properly, slouching around having moods. Look at it from her point of view. Her present life was very dull, an anticlimax to all the thrills of getting him here via 'the tiger-coloured stone', and seeing him win her hand in combat. But what could he do? You can't keep winning combats. A champion is best off as a challenger, so to speak, when everything is yet to be won. When everything *is* won the true tedium of life reveals itself. He shouldn't begrudge her Hubert's attentions.

His conscience troubled him over Miss Wingbone, too, although surely being transported to another universe was grounds enough for breaking off an engagement. Visiting Waldo's room frequently, he met her quite often. Waldo would tactfully withdraw, and he could speak in private.

'In the circumstances,' he said gravely – she was at arm's length but completely unreachable – 'we ought to call it a day.'

'All right,' she said cheerfully. 'I hope you'll be very happy. Quite frankly, I do find her rather like the heroine of a comic opera. Seeing her with that chorus line that trails round with her, I'm always expecting her to break into a solo song-and-dance routine. But everyone to his taste.'

She had the advantage of being able to see Miranda whenever Waldo willed it. Miranda could only have seen her by going to Waldo's room, which she would never consent to do; Waldo (disguised in a black wig) was a mere squire. Jonah was put out by her cheerfulness. He preferred her to be angry and upset. He didn't like her to be glad to get rid of him.

Miss Wingbone was not glad, had he but known. She felt she'd been badly used. She would never give her feelings away, of course. She kept a steely control over her emotions. But she did *have* emotions to keep a steely control over.

She shook her head for the nth time. It was all past belief. But whatever the case, she still wanted Jonah back, more than she would have once thought possible. She had at one time managed him so easily that 'needing' him never arose.

She needed a second string, she reflected, like Miranda's Hubert.

She thought of Peacock.

Peacock, not having eaten anything for several weeks, was beginning to take on the appearance of a jerboa. He was a slender youth, handsome in a delicate way, with dark wavy hair which he wore rather long. He was not unlike Hubert, come to think of it. He even composed love songs. He did not sing them aloud in the office to the accompaniment of a lute, but kept them locked up in his briefcase. He intended to post them to Miss Wingbone, one day, unsigned. But not yet, because he kept adding improving touches to them.

Miss Wingbone stepped out of the coils of the Long Thing, which by now swirled in a pyramid up to her waist, and called Peacock into her office.

'Sit down, Peacock.'

She took off her tinted glasses.

It wasn't fair; the effect was touching. His eyes became misty; his face took on a look of dog-like devotion. Kindness and tenderness surged up in her.

She addressed a series of separate remarks to him, with long pauses.

'I've been watching you lately.

'You are not eating enough.

'I doubt if you're eating anything!

'It won't do.'

'No, Miss Wingbone.'

She hesitated as to whether to take his hand and decided against it. She spoke softly.

'Peacock, you ought to get yourself a girl-friend.'

'I've got one, Miss Wingbone.'

'Have you?' she said, taken aback. 'What is her name?'

'Sharon.'

'And what . . .' She was at a loss, and hardly knew what to say. 'I mean . . . what does she do? . . . I mean, what work, sort of thing?'

'She works in the library.'

'Oh. That must be nice for you. I mean, you like reading, don't you?'

He nodded, still looking dazed with adoration.

'Oh well . . . er . . . well, good . . .' She assumed a brisker tone. 'There's the question of your work, Peacock – '

She replaced her glasses. His face cleared.

'Miss Wingbone,' he said solemnly, as if to the priest at confession, 'I idealize you.'

'Oh,' said Miss Wingbone. She felt that she was losing her grip on this conversation. 'Well. What does Sharon think about that?'

'She's all for it.'

'Oh?'

'She thinks it's good to idealize someone. A lot of people do – they idealize pop stars and footballers and that. Sharon thinks it's good for you to have someone to focus your daydreams on. She says it clears your mind of them and makes you fitter for the realities of life.'

'And what are the realities of life?'

'She doesn't say.'

'Plays safe, doesn't she? So I'm a kind of symbol? Isn't that just a trifle cold-blooded?'

She could see that he did not understand. He stared at her, almost smugly.

'Here,' she said, and produced a slice of cake, '*eat* this, now. Don't frame it.'

'That,' she said to herself, when he had gone, 'was the strangest conversation I've ever held.

'Symbol, am I?

'It seems to me,' she said to herself, 'that I'm missing out all along the line.'

CHAPTER EIGHT

The Lord Chamberlain was not pleased with Jonah's success. He would have preferred False Sir Topas to this newcomer. He could handle Sir Topas. The new knave was too cunning by half, and so was his squire. Until now the Lord Chamberlain had been easily the cleverest person in the palace, and he didn't like being relegated to third.

A natural sceptic, he was suspicious of their claims. Jonah's 'squire' looked to him uncommonly like the mad magician, Waldo, wearing a black wig. He doubted whether Jonah really came 'from far-off lands'. He thought it more likely that he came from quite nearby lands, and was, with his similar build, in all probability Waldo's cousin or even brother. Doubtless magic ran in the family.

That fight had been crooked if ever he'd seen one.

He would investigate. Mad Waldo couldn't be in two places at once.

Stuffing his pockets with coloured beads to offer to any wodwo that might accost him, and taking with him a young goat to allay the ravening of the chance two-headed worm, the prudent fellow made his way to the wood and sought out Waldo's hut. 'Mad Waldo is agone for the nones,' intoned a voice in answer to his knock. When he found that the hut was empty, he was considerably frightened, but he was a man of resolute nerve, and knocked again. 'Mad Waldo is agone for the nones,' repeated the voice with exactly the same intonation as before. The Lord Chamberlain found that, by knocking before the message was completed, he could make it repeat a bit from the middle:

'. . . thou mayst leave him word,' asserted the voice smoothly. He knocked. The voice hiccupped and recapitulated: '– leave him word. Stateth first –' He gave the door a stiff kick. This had the effect of making it repeat itself over and over again:

'. . . hight, and eke speaketh thy . . .
. . . hight, and eke speaketh thy . . .
. . . hight, and eke speaketh thy . . .'

His suspicions were now fully aroused. 'This is a wicked device that feigneth his presence,' he muttered. 'The villain is elsewhere . . .'

From now on he kept a close watch on Jonah's squire's room. It was always locked, but that was no problem, for he had a duplicate key to every room in the palace. Sooner or later Jonah's squire, who he was sure was Waldo, would slink back to the hut in the wood to see whether his speaking device had collected any messages. This bit of reasoning shows how bright the Lord Chancellor was. He was not quite top-drawer, though. A bit off-white, as we shall see.

Sure enough, the squire did creep away early one evening. Jonah, meanwhile, was being forced to sit with Miranda and her ladies and listen to a poet reciting a poem about romance and roses, which looked like going on for ever. The coast was clear. Trembling with anticipation, the Lord Chamberlain slipped into the squire's room.

It was like a hall of mirrors, with his own face looking at him from every angle. In the middle, on a table, was a cone-shaped thing that twirled round endlessly to no apparent purpose, rather like the poem that Jonah was being made to listen to. He was disappointed. He had expected crucibles, alembics, salamanders and skulls. Here was the sort of trash used by charlatans at fairs to bedazzle village maidens and their swains.

So you see he was not super-intelligent. The trouble was, he was a sceptic. Sceptics often fail to grasp what's under their noses.

He was about to leave when he noticed a piece of paper on a side table. On it was drawn a large square, broken up into much smaller squares, black and white, and arranged in a pattern. The white squares had letters in them. Underneath the big square was some writing, in lines of different length, making no sense whatever. The Lord Chamberlain saw that each line of words was preceded by a number, and (which seemed to him all the more sinister) also *followed* by a number in brackets, e.g:

2. Cyril composed the words of this song. (5)

He now noticed that the numbers to the left of each batch of words corresponded to numbers in the corners of the smaller white squares. Checking up number 2, for instance, he found five white squares in each of which had been written a letter. The five letters made up a word:

LYRIC

The astute reader, knowing about crosswords, will see that 'lyric' is an anagram of 'Cyril'. Waldo had seen it too. He delighted in this new game, and would persuade Miss Wingbone to read out *The Times* crossword to him, while he copied it down in his own handwriting and solved it as fast as he could write. But the Lord

Chamberlain, although commendably bright, was not equal to this; he was (as it were) clueless. Here, he decided, was cryptic magic. Find the key to this, and the fiendish secret of Jonah and his squire would be made plain. But of course no honest person would try to do so. It might summon the devil himself.

Anyway, the meaning didn't matter. What did matter was the fact that it existed at all. It could be used to demonstrate that Jonah and his squire were false, falser than false, and that Sir Topas had been beaten by trickery.

Demonstrated to whom, though? The king wouldn't listen, not after winning back all that he'd lost. Sir Topas? Sir Topas, although good at slicing kerchiefs in two, was rather thick. Taking the Lord Chamberlain for a king's man, he would probably hack him to pieces before he had a chance to speak. In any case, Jonah seemed able to beat him and his army single-handed.

The Lord Chamberlain crept back to his own room at the top of the west tower. From here he could see a wide stretch of Sudonian countryside, terminating, as far as the eye could reach, in the squalid holdings where the peasantry grovelled in their hovels.

His long thin nose twitched with disdain as he watched a distant churl, bowed down under a huge load of faggots, stumbling home in the lurid light of the setting sun.

There were thousands such, he reflected. They dragged out from day to day a living death.

Then his eye kindled. Thousands of them, all totally gullible, all capable of being roused to blind fury by tales of hanky-panky in high places!

There were his allies. The mob!

Miss Wingbone sat down at her desk. The coils of the Long Thing threatened to engulf her, as the coils of the worm had threatened Jonah in the Sudonian wood. She pushed it aside, and, fishing the morning's *Times* from her hold-all, glanced briefly at the crossword. Doing the crossword with Waldo was one of her few pleasures in a worried life, because he was so good at it, and could solve all the clues at once except those involving quotations. Then, as was her custom, she skimmed through the rest of the paper.

In the financial section there was a big, black, full-page advertisement for Towpath Ltd, arrogantly demanding the wealth of investors to help them take over Sprockett's Electricals. They were spending millions on this campaign. They looked like winning, too.

Something else occurred to her.

Towpath – Topas. Topas, Ltd. False Sir Towpath . . . The names were much alike, were they not?

Then a stream of comparisons rushed through her head. She looked at the Long Thing and thought of the Sudonian worm. She envisaged Peacock in the outer office and thought of the love-sick Hubert. She thought of tall, thin Jonah and compared him with tall, thin Waldo. She thought of Miranda and compared her with that piece who had played Cinderella in the pantomime. Parallels?

Miss Wingbone took off her glasses, chewed the side-piece, and gave up her powerful mind to profound thought.

Jonah, just before all this had begun, had been very depressed. He had found all the uses of this world weary, stale, flat and unprofitable. He had described it as loathsome. Clearly, he didn't like it much. Nor did he like himself. Hadn't he said something or other to his psychiatrist about being *taken out of himself*?

He would have liked to opt out.

Into a dream-world? Sudonia was just like a dream-world. Perpetual summer, a beautiful princess in distress, a gift of magic to defeat invincible foes . . .

And what was more, it was vague, as one would expect of a dream-world. It seemed to have no geography apart from a wood, a stream, a daisied bank or two. It seemed to have no history apart from scraps of information about a feckless king and false knights. It seemed to have no commerce, no craftsmen's guilds, no middle classes. It had a mixed-up language – which incidentally was English, very convenient for Jonah, and very unexpected in an alien universe – a mixed-up language made up of speech from various centuries. Vague, Sudonia was, as vague as you would expect the daydream to be of someone who had romantic yearnings and hadn't read much.

Jonah hadn't read much . . .

Miss Wingbone chewed the other side-piece and reflected on Jonah's childhood.

His mother had read him fairy stories.

His father had played games with him with wooden swords.

He had loved his parents, and they had loved him, but actors' marriages are often insecure, and when he was ten years old they had split up. They had gone on being nice to each other, like civilized people, but the break-up had been a terrific shock to Jonah, so that from then on he had read nothing but technical books.

To be sure, he had read them to advantage. He had grown up to be a great engineer. But that itself had brought its troubles. Great success is hard to live with. Where do you go when you've won everything?

Into a dream-world. A dream-world made up of the memories of childhood.

And Jonah, the man of genius, seemed to have made his dream-world real.

In doing which, he erred, reflected Miss Wingbone sadly. Peacock and Hubert had more sense than he. It is miserable enough to wake up from a beautiful dream to cold reality, but more miserable still to keep on dreaming till the dream itself becomes cold reality. Poor Jonah was heading for disillusionment . . .

Yes, yes, yes, said Miss Wingbone, pulling herself up short, this amateur psychology is all very well, but it won't do. Sudonia is not a dream. I have seen it, it's really there, green sward, cloud-capped towers and all, with Waldo ready to do the latest crossword, much better than Jonah could ever manage . . .

At which point another comparison struck her, more poignant even than the others. Was not Waldo, with his ridiculously high IQ and his talent for crosswords, just like a projection of Jonah himself, a Jonah wish-fulfilled?

She chewed so hard on the side-piece of her glasses that a bit snapped off in her mouth. She spat it out crossly and lost track of her bewildering thoughts.

One hears of dreams coming true, it's a cliché, but Jonah was surely the first man in history to make it happen in literal fact. However had he done that? By accident? With mirrors?

She shook her head. She could not answer that.

The Lord Chamberlain had decided that he must woo the mob by means of oratory, and he practised in his own room for a bit to get the right approach. At first he opened his practice speeches with such words as, 'Listen to me, you dogs,' or, simply, 'Rabble!' – but he decided on reflection that these might lack the common touch. Something more ingratiating was needed. 'My friends'? Yes, that was good. Plain and straightforward. But then he had to work on his facial expression, so as not to appear about to vomit when he spoke.

Getting in touch with the mob was no problem, because it was one of his duties to order the festivities for Miranda's wedding, which entailed commanding the common folk to hang bunting outside their hovels, and line the streets in joyful but orderly crowds. Drilling them into being both joyful and orderly was going to take a long time, and he had already despatched troops of soldiers to different places to knock their shambling legions into shape.

Travelling several leagues to the largest of the village greens, and using the stocks at the edge of it for a platform, he held up his hand for silence, and began addressing them:

'My dear friends – '

Shifty, sidelong glances, surly murmurs. The crowd-noises of this crowd, who had never heard of rhubarb, sounded like a consortium of their own pigs.

'. . . My dear friends, as you know, our beloved princess – '

Ah, at that, they knew what was expected of them. Hurrah, hurrah! Bless her! Hurrah!

'Quite so. Bless her,' said the Lord Chamberlain, impatient at the interruption. 'Our beloved princess is to be married, as you know, to the knight from far-off lands, Jonah of the Sprockett Hasp!'

The pace in Sudonia, as we have seen, was very leisurely, and the cheering of the crowd was now so prolonged that it threatened to compete with Hubert's swoon in length. The Lord Chamberlain became downright irritable.

'All right, all right, that's enough!' he snapped.

'Sergeant! If anyone continues cheering, crop his ears!'

A long, low, subsiding growl from the crowd.

'Jonah of the Sprockett Hasp,' continued the Lord Chamberlain, keeping a menacing eye on the squat figures before him, 'is great in arms. He must be, to beat False Sir Topas and a score of his knights without receiving a scratch! How did he do it? Was it sheer might of arms? Or was it . . . *something else*?'

Dead silence.

'You may discuss this among yourselves.'

The crowd obliged. 'Sheer might of arms? Couldn't have been. Something else? Must've been. But what? That's what we want to know!' Cynical interrogative growling.

'It has been suggested,' went on the Lord Chamberlain, 'that our friend from distant lands used *magic* – I repeat, *magic* – to gain his victory! You will tell me, this is a vile rumour – '

Yes, it's a vile rumour! It's a vile rumour, we tell you!

'Dear friends, so I thought myself! So I thought myself! But *then* – in the chamber of Jonah's squire – I came upon – I came upon – a piece of paper! *This* piece of paper!'

Grim, sidelong glances, and some snarling. The mob detested education.

'It is a wicked piece of paper! A damning document! A vile inscription! Oh my friends, were I to read it to you . . . But I dare not! It might turn you against the noble knight who is to marry our beloved princess!'

Read it, read it! Noble knight? Ha ha! he is a villain!

'My friends, this document,' said the Lord Chamberlain, dropping his voice to a thrilling quietness, 'is one of the most damnable ever penned by perverted mankind instructed by fiends. It is a mass of wicked words interlaced. If I read it aloud it would kill yourselves and

75

me stone dead on this spot. And if it could do that to you, hardy, strong men that you are, what would it do to a delicately nurtured, innocent girl?'

Before they could decide what could be worse than being struck dead on the spot, the Lord Chamberlain continued:

'I hope you will restrain yourselves, dear friends. I hope you will not resort to violence. I hope you will choke down your very natural, loyal, manly anger. I know you all feel like seizing clubs, staves, pickaxe handles and the legs of chairs and storming the palace to rescue our princess from the scoundrels who have her in thrall – but I beg you to resist this urge – great-hearted though it is – '

He could go no further, because the crowd, shouting, 'Let us take clubs, staves, pickaxe handles and chair-legs and rescue our princess from those scoundrels,' rushed about like an overturned anthill, and when they had armed themselves, began pouring in a thunderous flood in the direction of the palace. 'Our urge is great-hearted,' they bellowed, as they went.

The Lord Chamberlain, sucking a throat lozenge, watched them with dark satisfaction. It had been child's play, and he hadn't had to waste blank verse on them, either.

He would have been all the more satisfied had he known that that sword of Jonah's wouldn't be any use against weapons made of wood.

CHAPTER NINE

It was not, however, so straightforward as he had expected.

Several leagues lay between the mob and the palace, and long before they had covered half that distance they ceased to be a thunderous flood. Some simply got out of breath; others recalled that their wives expected them home to tea. The evening sun was mellowing behind the hills, it would soon be dark, the palace drawbridge would be up and they didn't fancy swimming the moat. Some gave up and went home, but the majority bivouacked for the night and arranged to draw up a proper plan of attack for the next day.

And of course complications set in. For one thing, the farmer in whose fields they bivouacked resented their presence, and, aided by fellow farmers and their hands, attacked them with dogs and cudgels, and a great brawl ensued. Eventually they found a clearing in the woods where they could settle in peace, but by now their first fury had subsided and they began to demand leadership and strategy, and to bicker amongst themselves.

Soon they were no longer a united mob, but broken up into quarrelsome factions. Some were all for charging on as fast as they could and rescuing the princess before it was too late. The question 'too late for what?'

drove them mad. Hair-splitting, nit-picking, while the first lady of the realm was in peril? Hesitate now, and all the womanhood of Sudonia was at risk. They made fiery speeches against wishy-washy speechifying, and bashed those who disagreed with them.

Some, on the other hand, said that if they rushed at the thing too hastily the princess would be in even greater danger, because the villains who held her in thrall would be panicked into doing her mortal harm. They wanted to discuss matters at length, and kept forming committees.

And then there was a third group of wretches, the barrack-room lawyer kind, who cast doubt on the whole enterprise. They picked holes in the Lord Chamberlain's speech. If the piece of paper could kill people on the spot, why hadn't it killed him? And if he hadn't dared to read it, how did he know what was in it? Not being quite sure what they were grumbling about, they worked up a great grievance about that piece of paper, declaring their right to see it. They attracted a large following of people who had been at the back of the mob and hadn't been able to hear what the Lord Chamberlain was saying, but became convinced that to see that piece of paper would transform their lives.

There was a fourth group who quickly and efficiently formed themselves into a robber band. It had to be said that these were the most enterprising and intelligent of them all. They dedicated themselves to robbing the rich, which was sound good sense, as there's not much percentage in robbing the poor. In later years, past the time of this story, they became quite legendary, and attracted respectable persons to their ranks, including a miller's son and even a friar. They took to wearing attractive green clothes and were dab hands with hunting horns.

Meanwhile, with all these distractions, the uprising was not getting anywhere. Or rather it was, but extremely slowly, as the sea encroaches upon the land. Distant encampments began to be visible from the palace itself. A rumble of uncouth talk drifted across the palatial grounds and imposed itself upon the sounds of lutes and the recitations of poems about roses. The Lord Chamberlain kept looking out of his chamber window and fretting. Life in Sudonia moved slowly, yes, but this was ridiculous.

At last he decided to do something about it in person. He went alone this time, deeming troops unnecessary, and in order not to stress his wealth too heavily, wore only a few rings, necklaces and bracelets, a quilted doublet slashed with gold, and some casual, jewel-studded sandals. He rode a white palfrey with a saddle-cloth of crimson, with gold tassels.

He had gone only a league into the wilds when he encountered the robber band, who lifted him from his horse with great courtesy, and, holding him firmly by the arms, addressed him in song. They had already foreseen that in the future, people would write musicals about them, and they wanted to leave some jolly rebel songs to be included in these. Besides, their leader had a fine baritone voice of which he was very proud. It was he who addressed the Lord Chamberlain, in these words:

> Pardon me, sir,
> I'm sorry to detain you,
> But surely it's unwise
> To roam this wicked region
> In jewels of such enormous size?

Here the robbers joined in the chorus:

You'd better let us take care of them;
There's danger in so much wealth;
　　　You might run into a robber band,
And we're anxious about your health.

The robbers gently relieved the Lord Chamberlain of his jewellery, and their leader sang another stanza:

Pardon me, sir,
　　I'm sorry to detain you,
　　　But isn't it indiscreet
　　　　To wear such costly sandals
　　On your refined and shapely feet?
Chorus: You'd better let us, etc.

The robbers removed the Lord Chamberlain's sandals, and their leader sang again:

Pardon me, sir,
　　I'm sorry to detain you,
　　　But isn't it rash of you
　　　　To roam this wicked region
　　In robes of such resplendent hue?
Chorus: You'd better let us, etc.

The robbers took off the Lord Chamberlain's clothes, and their leader, who was in excellent voice and just getting into his stride, began yet another stanza:

Pardon me, sir,
　　I'm sorry to detain you,
　　　But in the normal course
　　　　Of gentlemanly breeding
　　We'll tender your class-conscious horse –

But now the robbers, who were getting tired of singing 'etc.', and knew that their leader would go on for another fifty stanzas if they let him, pointedly walked away, leading the Lord Chamberlain with them.

The following morning a lone archer appeared on the outskirts of the palace and shot an arrow with a message attached to it. It fell into the moat. After a number of similar unsuccessful shots, he gave up, and delivered his message in semaphore to the lords and ladies who had gathered on the battlements to watch him. They had difficulty in following him and told one another laughingly that they'd done this stuff at school but had got a bit rusty; but in the end they worked out the message. It stated that the Lord Chamberlain was being held to ransom, and named an enormous sum. If this were not delivered within a certain time they would start despatching various portions of his anatomy to the palace, beginning with his left ear.

The king took this kidnapping seriously, for he relied on the Lord Chamberlain for many services. There was no immediate hurry, of course, because the Lord Chamberlain could do his work as well with one ear as with two, but something would have to be done before they dismantled him completely.

He sent in his troops. This was a fiasco. They were not used to guerrilla warfare; their foes always met them in the open field, lumbering towards them in the most accessible fashion. This time they could not locate the foe at all to begin with, and were drawn to them only by the sound of a song they were singing, deep in the woods, about how merry life was in the greenwood. When they tried to plough their way into the woods the branches knocked them off their horses, and when they went on foot their spurs got snarled in roots and twigs got stuck in the interstices of their visors. The robbers watched them clanking about and went on singing. They did not shoot at them, because it was such a nuisance to collect up the arrows afterwards; and so this conflict resembled Jonah's fight with False Sir Topas, in that it was a triumph of non-resistance. In the end the soldiers gave up in a huff and limped home.

The Princess Miranda now made a suggestion. Why not invite the Knight of the Sprockett Hasp to do the job? This was the sort of thing he could do single-handed before breakfast, bringing the robbers back roped together in bunches of twelve.

She put it to her father eagerly, because she was growing rather tired of Jonah in inactivity. He did not dance or sing, stared gloomily at the ground while listening to recitations, and when presented with single roses, eyed them with resignation. Her ladies were already calling him 'the knight of the doleful visage'. Miranda decided that he was happy only when engaged in violent action, and she hoped that when they were married he would take himself off on foreign campaigns and do noble deeds in her honour far away and for the longest possible stretches of time. So far from recognizing his great intellect, she secretly thought him rather stupid. When they had first met he had been like a landed fish, and he had gone about nonplussed ever since.

Jonah accepted the task – he could hardly do otherwise – but with much misgiving. Where would this sort of thing have an end? He had supposed that once you had married the girl of your dreams you lived happily ever after. He now foresaw being condemned to a lifetime of foolhardy exploits. He did not like the idea of playing hide-and-seek in the woods with robbers, and he didn't want to rescue the Lord Chamberlain anyway. He didn't like the way the man looked at him, with his weaselly face.

Instinctively his hand went to his pocket in search of

The Times crossword, his old source of relief in times of perplexity. But of course it wasn't there, and even if it had been, no good would have come of it, because Waldo solved all the clues now before he himself even understood the wording of them. Shocked at himself, but wistfully nevertheless, Jonah wished he could be back on earth with Miss Wingbone, having tiffs about anagrams and the like.

Waldo was a tremendous ally, but he obviously had an axe to grind. He spent every spare moment contacting Miss Wingbone, lapping up the crosswords, and straining every fibre to enter her world. And sooner or later he would succeed. With a brain like his he was bound to. What a prospect: Waldo home and dry with Miss Wingbone and Sprockett's Electricals, and he, Jonah, stranded here with Miranda and an endless round of heroic deeds!

'Stranded'! Jonah could see the irony of this, and smiled wryly at himself. But once you have stopped being infatuated, you can't imagine why you ever were, and what he had felt about Miranda now had no meaning for him. She bored him. So soon.

Then, reminding himself that he could no more get out of marrying her than he could get out of Sudonia itself, he tried to convince himself that he didn't really feel like that at all; just moody, he was. Yes, that was it. Moody. You couldn't help being moody. 'I am life's victim,' he groaned.

All the while, he was grimly aware, the robbers lay in the wood, planning the vivisection of the Lord Chamberlain.

Whenever he had been in a tight corner before, he had turned for help to Miss Wingbone. Could he, in all conscience, do so now? Ask her to help him clear up a little matter on his way to marriage with someone else?

Yes, as a matter of fact, he probably could. He felt ashamed, but he went ahead all the same.

Waldo had now devised a button by the side of the revolving cone, which, when pressed, called up Miss Wingbone in her flat. Human beings do not retain a sense of wonder for long, and now, whenever she heard the warning buzz, she just said to herself, 'That'll be Waldo,' as if it were no more than a telephone call, and not a miraculous summons from another universe. And why not? The telephone is just as much a miracle, in its way.

But this time it was not Waldo but Jonah, gangling in an embroidered jerkin from his now extensive wardrobe, and looking sheepish. Waldo had tactfully left him alone for this interview.

Miss Wingbone was more pleased to see Jonah than he could have ever imagined, but she always hid her feelings, with especial success when she was wearing her dark glasses. 'Well, well,' she said drily, appearing in the magic doorway and looking inscrutably at Jonah as, having faltered out his case, he stood awaiting her comment, the cone spreading sickly waves of light over his face, 'can't the Princess Miranda give you any advice?'

'I haven't asked her.'

'Ah. More for ornament than use, is she?'

'Look – '

'Yes, yes. Well. This is a two-pipe problem, Jonah . . . Can you use a bow and arrow?'

'If you think I'm going to – '

'No, of course I don't. On no account go into the wood and on no account try to fight them in any way. Now I come to think of it, you've told me that you used to play with bows and arrows with your father when you were a little boy. That'll do. Now, do you

84

think you could make a magnetic target?'

'Yes, I should think so ... *Target*? What are you talking about?'

'I'm not sure yet. I shall have to work it out. Keep in touch.'

'But, really – '

'Say, this time tomorrow?'

'All right.' Jonah swallowed. 'And – thanks.'

'Don't mention it.'

Miss Wingbone returned to her kitchen and finished off a cup of cold coffee.

'I am a stooge,' she said. 'I'm a symbol for Peacock and a kind of trainer-manager for Jonah, and for what? To help their love-lives run smoothly! Isn't it marvellous! As a person in my own right, I just don't exist!'

The words 'don't exist' echoed in her head. Did Sudonia exist? – or had Jonah and his mirror really created it out of his own imagination? That was her own theory, and because we all believe far more strongly in theories than in facts she stuck to it.

'Things don't look too good, though,' she remarked. 'I'm afraid he's letting his imagination run away with him.'

CHAPTER TEN

A day or two later the robbers were in their camp, singing their merry song about life in the greenwood, but with rather diminished gusto. They were finding it hard to hunt for food – the woodland animals, witnessing their efforts with bows and arrows, just walked away – and they had as yet to find a buyer for what they had stolen from the Lord Chamberlain. They needed money so that they could go into the shops and buy food. Stealing it was difficult, because they had sworn not to rob from the poor, and the rich all lived in impregnable castles.

They were treating the Lord Chamberlain as courteously as was compatible with tying him to a tree and feeding him on grass.

They were disturbed by the sound of footsteps, and in a moment Mad Waldo stood before them, his straw-like hair shorter than usual, but otherwise his unchanged self, monk's habit, wild blue eyes and all. They greeted him warmly. Most of them had been to his hut for simples at some time or other.

'Sit down and eat, and welcome to our table,' said the robber chief.

Waldo took one look at the nettle soup. 'No thank you,' he said, but he did sit down. 'Now then,' he said, 'you good sportsmen love a gamble, don't you?'

'Not really,' said the robber chief, exchanging doubtful glances with his men. 'We don't like losing.'

'Ah. But you would gamble on a certainty?'

'Ye-es, but then it wouldn't be gambling.'

Waldo had news for them. The king, that inveterate gambler, was ready to do a deal. Realizing that his soldiers had no chance of rescuing the Lord Chamberlain, he was willing to risk everything on a wager – the return of the Lord Chamberlain, unharmed, if they lost; the payment of three times the ransom if they won.

'Three times our ransom demand! We could set ourselves up as a Limited Company! We could take out a mortgage on a castle! Imagine sleeping in real beds again, lads . . . Here, where's the catch?'

'No catch. Your champion against the Knight of the Sprockett Hasp.'

'Oh no. There's something fishy about that sword of his. False Sir Topas was framed.'

'Not swords: archery.'

A roar of laughter greeted this. 'You picked the wrong men,' said the robber chief. 'Have you seen us with bows and arrows? We couldn't hit the side of the king's palace! Even the rabbits round here think we're rabbits.'

'Don't be so sure,' said Waldo mysteriously. He picked up a tiny yellow leaf, walked twenty paces away, and stuck it carefully to the trunk of a tree. 'Hit that,' he invited the robber chief.

'You're joking.'

'Try it.'

Shrugging, and with much chuckling, the robber chief fitted an arrow to his bow and loosed it. It was a bad shot, the arrow wobbling and the feathers vibrating. At least, for a few yards it was. Then the arrow steadied itself, flew straight and hard, and hit the tiny leaf right in the centre.

'And you can do that,' said Waldo, 'every time.'

'It's magic,' said the robber chief hoarsely.

'Of course it's magic.'

There was now a rush by all the robbers to have a go. They selected small fragments for targets – leaves, berries, the petals of tiny flowers. Waldo took charge of each fragment, fixing it carefully to the same tree. Each time the arrow, no matter how uncertainly loosed, plunged accurately to the very heart of the spot aimed at.

'Try it blindfold,' said Waldo.

The robber chief suffered himself to be blindfolded and split a piece of straw in two at fifty paces.

'I'd call it a dead cert, wouldn't you?' said Waldo. He held up a small metal ring. 'This is the secret. You push this into the bull and your arrow is bound to pass through it. It's spiked on the other side, see? You can't miss. You must win.'

'How are we to get near the butt?'

'Post one of your lads there to pull your arrows out for you.'

'Why are you helping us?'

'Am I not a man of the woods, like you?'

'Ex-man of the woods,' said the robber chief doubtfully. 'That hut of yours has got a ghost in it. I don't like the sound of this. How do we know we shan't be walking into a trap?'

'The king always honours a bet.'

'We shall check up on what you've said.'

'Check up all you like. You'll get an official challenge from the palace soon. Mind how much you lop off the Lord Chamberlain. Keep him intact.'

'Just what's in all this for you, Mad Waldo?'

'I shall expect to be made a shareholder in your limited company.'

'Verily,' said the robber chief, moved to talk posh, which was generally against his principles, 'an't come about, we shall be swift to require your gentillesse. We shall be much beholden to you, in sooth.'

'Be my guest,' said Mad Waldo.

'This is hardly honest,' said Jonah.

Waldo found Jonah's strict regard for truthfulness rather embarrassing. 'We are good,' he said, not for the first time. 'That makes it all right.'

'But can one hide the truth and still be good?'

'You should not trouble yourself with such questions. They probably cause that depression of yours.'

King Bevis was in no two moods about it. To gamble and be certain of winning was to have the best of two worlds. He did not know what scheme Jonah and his squire had devised, but he knew it involved magic, and he had great faith in it. He sent out heralds to issue the challenge to the robbers, and as soon as he received their reply, delivered in shaky semaphore, he tried to place as many side bets as he could. A remarkably large number of people were ready to bet against Jonah. The rumour had gone round that the robbers were wonderful bowmen who could split a single straw at fifty paces, and that if Jonah landed an arrow in the centre of the bull, the robber chief would split his shaft with his next shot.

Miss Wingbone, 'switched on' by Waldo, was a secret but keen spectator of the contest. She had taken an afternoon off from work to watch it. It was her own idea; she had far more business ability than Jonah. All he had to do was to make one or two inventions on her instructions; one might say (although it would be confusing in this case) that she made the bolts and let him fire them. We must not forget the important part played by Waldo, of course. But this can be even more confusing, if you lean to Miss Wingbone's thinking; she believed that Waldo *was* Jonah, a kind of ideal self dreamed up. The reader is advised to reserve his judgement on this baffling theory for the time being, and concentrate on the rigged archery contest.

Once again the great field in the king's grounds was thronged with lords and ladies, except that False Sir Topas and his knights were absent. Ever since their crushing defeat by Jonah they had skulked in Sir Topas's castle, not daring to show their faces. There were several preliminary events, including jousting, tumbling, wrestling, and a ladies' egg-and-spoon race; but in due time these were all disposed of, the archery bulls were set up, and the contestants entered the field.

The robbers brought the Lord Chamberlain with them, not risking leaving him tied to his tree for fear that he might be stolen from them by some gang with no moral scruples. He was unbound – there was no danger of his trying to escape or being rescued, because in Sudonian polite society, bets were sacred – but they had not given him back his costly clothes. He was clad in an ill-fitting smock and could have been mistaken for a competitor in the sack-race.

A herald introduced the two opponents and lots were drawn for the order of shooting. Jonah won, and chose to shoot second. One of the robber band went down to the butt and, on the pretext of examining it, pressed the magic ring firmly into the bull. The robber chief, looking the picture of confidence, loosed his first shaft. His bowstring twanged like a jew's harp; his arrow oscillated so much that ten arrows seemed to hang in the air;

but then it sped straight to the target. It was a good shot, but not perfect. He had scored an inner, his arrow lodging just outside the rim of the bull.

The assistant robber, looking just a little disappointed, retrieved the arrow and palmed the magic ring, and Waldo, disguised in his black wig, inspected the target in his turn. The audience sniggered at these manoeuvrings, but goodnaturedly enough. Waldo had concealed a second magic ring in his palm; he pressed it to the centre of the bull; Jonah shot. His arrow did not vibrate like the robber chief's, but sailed languidly into the air and seemed about to drop feebly to the ground about halfway, but then it acquired new life, developed a high-pitched whine, and rammed itself so deeply into the very centre of the bull that Waldo had to bring his foot into play to tug it out.

The assistant robber went through the same ritual as before, and the robber chief, pursing his lips, shot again. Once more he scored a commendable inner, and Jonah, after due preliminaries, once again scored a perfect bull.

The robber chief now strode fuming down to the butt and began an altercation with his assistant. He seemed to be accusing him of having fumbled his work in some way; the assistant, with equal heat, seemed to be swearing that he had not. While Jonah waited patiently and Waldo, only a few paces away, pretended not to hear, the two carried on with raised voices and even threatening gestures. Finally the assistant robber flung something to the ground and stormed off in a huff, and the robber chief, with no attempt at concealment, picked up the magic ring and rammed it into the centre of the bull, stepping back to study it with scowling care before returning to his place.

The audience treated him to loud laughter and jeers.

They knew quite well that magical trickery was afoot. Unostentatiously though Waldo and the robber had pushed home the magic rings, they had not been entirely able to conceal the fact that they were tampering with the target. Moreover, arrows did not recover themselves in midflight after all but flopped on to the grass, nor did they turn almost at right angles in the air to get on course. They were not shocked to see the strong rumour confirmed that Jonah was a magician; they liked him for being a successful one. There was another rumour that the robber chief had been consorting with the madman of the woods, Waldo, who certainly had a trick or two up his sleeve; well, this time Waldo had met his match! Ha ha ha! Peace: the varlet shooteth.

The robber chief was in such a bad temper that this time he scarcely tried to take aim. His twanging arrow started off in the direction of the audience to his right, causing them to duck low, laughing gleefully; then it righted itself, and, to everyone's delight, sailed up to the target and scored another inner.

There was no one down there now to retrieve his arrow. He hesitated for a moment, snarling. The contest was on a best-of-five basis, so technically he was not yet defeated, but he did not wait for Jonah's next shot. Forgetting all about being courteous, he stormed off, snapping his fingers at his men to follow him, and leaving the Lord Chamberlain, looking like a discarded mail bag, alone in the field.

Prolonged, ecstatic applause. The Knight of the Sprockett Hasp had done it again. The king rushed up to Jonah and kissed him on both cheeks. Miranda, more decorously, took his hand, curtsied, and handed him a rose, wondering meanwhile how long it would be before the next deed of arms. Jonah bowed to all the points of the compass. Waldo pulled out the robber chief's magic ring from the target and strolled up, jingling both rings in his pocket.

The Lord Chamberlain, meanwhile, was glad not to be tied to a tree and stuffed with grass any more, but he was not happy by any means. For one thing he had lost his rings and his clothes; for another it was humiliating to have been captured by such a bungling lot as the robbers had turned out to be. But above all it was utterly galling to be rescued by Jonah. The Lord Chamberlain himself had in a way set the whole thing up by trying to do Jonah down, and look what a mess he had made of it.

The reader will have guessed the secret of the archery contest. The magic ring that Waldo had given the robbers worked perfectly well on an untreated surface, ensuring a bull's-eye every time. But the target used in the contest was also magnetized, in such a way as to render the robbers' ring slightly inaccurate, while Jonah, using a cunningly adjusted one, was able to hit the bull with mechanical precision.

A successful plan was Miss Wingbone's. She looked on the afternoon's work with satisfaction. Yet she knew that Jonah's problems were not over.

CHAPTER ELEVEN

After the archery contest, life in Sudonia seemingly settled down to normal. Jonah divided his time between attending Miranda and her ladies and lounging in his opulent suite of rooms, waited on by pages who peeled grapes for him and sang roundelays in piping trebles. Time hung heavy on his hands. He wished – reluctantly, against his own will, he wished – that he could be back on earth, dealing with silly women from Leeds who worried about dishwashers. He even began to feel an affection for Towpath, Ltd., who had given life (he now realized) a certain zest.

The Lord Chamberlain had the mortification of having to appear grateful to Jonah, and to keep smiling at the many people who congratulated him on his escape. Worse, he had to make a speech of thanks when the king presented Jonah with a gem-studded coronet. An experienced diplomat, he succeeded in speaking, smiling, and grinding his teeth at the same time.

Sir Topas, skulking in his castle, wondered whether there was any longer any point in being false, when the other lot, for goodness sake, could get away with so much. He had heard about the farcical archery contest, and he was now more certain than ever that his own fight had been fixed, but what could he do about it? Goodness was triumphant. It was all so unfair.

Meanwhile, there was one section of the mob roused by the Lord Chamberlain that had never given up their campaign, and they were getting nearer inch by inch. Looking out of the palace windows, courtiers could see a row of unkempt heads bobbing over the distant hedges.

Some inquired languidly, 'What are those shaggy ruffians about?'

Others rebuked them: 'Surely that question is not in the best of taste?'

But the Lord Chamberlain saw them with a flicker of hope.

After playing jack-in-the-boxes for some while, the mob moved forward into the open fields, chanting revolutionary slogans as they went:

> Let him fall into our grasp,
> That false Knight of the Sprockett Hasp!

It happened that the fields into which they moved forward cut across a corner of lands belonging to False Sir Topas, and soon one of his henchmen came to him to apprise him of this fact. Sir Topas had lost weight lately, and looked a little shrunken and bowed down, but immediately on hearing the news he swelled with rage. He jammed a helmet on his head and strode out to meet the trespassers, swishing his sword. A bluebottle that buzzed in a corridor fell in two halves behind him as he went. Scorning to call up his followers, he made his way alone to face the ugly, yelling swarm, stomping over the drawbridge in smoking fury. If that had not been hastily lowered in time by a rush of menials, he might well have swum across the moat and frightened the man-eating fish.

The mob crouched savagely at bay; or perhaps less savagely than in surly puzzlement. Had not False Sir

Topas been unfairly beaten in battle by Jonah's wicked magic? Didn't that in a manner of speaking put him on their side? Would it not therefore be hasty to batter him with their staves and pickaxe handles?

Their uncouth dialogue expressed this dilemma:

'Was not False Sir Topas beaten unfairly in battle by Sprockett Hasp's wicked magic?'

'So he was.'

'Does that not in a manner of speaking put him on our side?'

'So it does.'

'Would it not therefore be hasty to batter him with our staves and pickaxe handles?'

'So it would.'

Their dialogue being uncouth, Sir Topas could not understand it, but even if he could it would not have mattered. Pointing his sword at them, he said in level but grinding tones: 'I shall count ten. In that time you will leave my land and return to your noisome hovels. Anyone who is left will be carved into thin slices.'

The mob backed away, muttering, for Sir Topas even as a has-been was still much dreaded. That is, those in front backed away; those behind, a shapeless horde, were unaware of Sir Topas's presence, and pressed on, still bawling their mindless chant:

> When we catch him he will gasp,
> That false knight of the Sprockett Hasp!

As the front ranks subsided into a sullen silence, these words from the rear were heard by Sir Topas, and now he, too, wavered in his purpose.

'What's that they're saying?'

A score of mouths answered him, in accents coarse enough, but in words not unwelcome to his ear. The Knight of the Sprockett Hasp was false! He had won his bouts by the use of evil magic! They had this on the highest authority!

'Have ye, though!' marvelled Sir Topas. 'Any idea what a Sprockett Hasp is?'

'No, your honour.'

'Neither have I. Neither would any decent person have.'

'Belike it is some form of devilry, your worship.'

'Very like, very like. Ha! So that's why ye're tramping across my land. Rough justice, eh? Out to give him his deserts, are ye?'

'He will get his desserts, my lord, after we have given him his main course,' said one peasant, who, in a less rigid social system, would have become a professional clown, 'and we think that will go much against his stomach.'

'Ha! You are honest fellows. Don't worry about crossing my land. I'll show you a short cut. Follow me!'

And so it was that the courtiers saw the mob again, much nearer this time, for the Lord Chamberlain, hardly able to believe his good luck, had lowered the drawbridge, and they were swarming through the palace grounds themselves. Passing the field where Miranda was dancing in a ring with her ladies, they paused briefly to give her three cheers and sing the national anthem; then on they pelted in an uncontrollable wave.

Now they were raging through the palace itself. Well, no, 'raging' is not quite the word. The Lord Chamberlain, imposing in his state robes, had quelled them with his presence and taken charge, so that their progress now became more like the conducted tour of a stately home, except that he spent no time at all discussing carved balustrades or ornamental ceilings, but led them straight to Jonah's squire's room, where, packing every corridor, they waited till he turned the key. Sir Topas, now completely out of his depth, stood by, hardly able to raise his arms for the pressure of the teeming bodies around him. Waldo and Jonah, convinced that the mob meant no good, had taken refuge in the Lord Chamberlain's own chamber, the safest place in the palace. There is no record of what the king was doing. Having an afternoon sleep, perhaps.

It happened that Miss Wingbone, having spent that Saturday morning shopping, was trying on an immensely expensive new gown. She had bought several, and had passed the whole afternoon parading in them. Until now she had invariably worn severe tailor-made costumes, but she was getting dissatisfied with her own image, and had decided, with some misgiving, on a complete change of dress. She studied herself in her mirror, then in Jonah's, and was not displeased with the effect. The silver folds hung elegantly about her slender body. On an impulse, she let down her golden hair, which she usually wore tightly coiled, and shook it about her shoulders. She even blushed at the result, and put on her dark glasses as if in protection. Nevertheless, she felt, it would be agreeable if Waldo, or better still Jonah himself, were to call her up at this moment.

Which is precisely what happened, or rather, *im*precisely what happened.

The Lord Chamberlain's trouble was that he was too clever. The mob being so successfully on the rampage, he should have let them find Jonah and Waldo and lynch them, but he could not leave well alone, he must try for one more turn of the knife. So he packed as many of them as he could into Waldo's room, with the great mass of them outside filling every inch in defiance of fire regulations, and lectured them on the evils of the written word, while he searched in vain for another crossword puzzle to illustrate his argument.

And of course, they became bored, and fidgeted like children on an educational visit. They showed interest only in what the Lord Chamberlain considered the unimportant things, the showy trash. They dabbed at the spiralling cone, they pulled faces in the mirrors, and, finding that they moved, turned them this way and that. At last, by blind chance, one of them touched the button that was needed to call up Miss Wingbone, and in a sudden revelation a door opened in the opposite wall, and Miss Wingbone, glittering in a silver gown, her hair streaming about her shoulders, her huge glasses black and gleaming, appeared before them.

There was stunned silence for several seconds. The Lord Chamberlain had his back to her and was the last to see her. It is to his credit that he did not lose his nerve, although he was extremely frightened. He tried to turn the apparition to his advantage. 'A witch!' he shouted. 'There, there's proof of what I say! It is a witch from the infernal regions! Seize her!' And, thrusting the shuddering peasants aside, he strode boldly up to Miss Wingbone and tried to lay hands on her. But he could not. His hands strayed ineptly about, groping the air, grasping nothing. She, like a cat taunting a chained-up dog, kept still, and as cold as ice.

Those in the room were seized by mad, uncontrollable terror. 'A Witch!' they yelled, and punched and kicked and trampled one another to get out. Those in the corridors, after looking blank and asking, foolishly, 'A what?' became infected with the panic, and soon the whole horde was thundering down the corridors of the palace with a roar like Niagara. Sir Topas was swept along with them, his arms pinned, his sword useless, and flung down a flight of stairs, and pitched over a balcony into a courtyard where he lay unconscious, the mob trampling his body as they poured after him. The Lord Chamberlain was even less fortunate. Caught up in the slipstream, he was swung along through corridors, down stairs, and across courtyards, till the mob reached the drawbridge itself, during which time his feet never touched the ground. On the drawbridge, by chance, he was twisted to the edge and pitched into the moat, where, being unable to swim, he drowned.

Miss Wingbone looked round Waldo's vacated room. The cone still maintained its eternal spiral and, incredibly enough, the mirrors on the walls still hung in place, just as cups will hang unbroken on the wall in a building shattered by a bomb. On the floor lay one hapless peasant, stunned, and bleeding from the nose. She spoke to him compassionately.

'There's nothing to be afraid of. See if you can stand up. Gently, now.'

He looked up at her, stupefied, his eyes glazed and bloodshot. Terror blazed in them. He sprang up, too soon, too quickly, and reeled and fell. He fell with a crash against the table bearing the cone. He did what the stampeding mob had not done: he knocked it over. The cone jumped, fizzed like a firework, rolled loose and became detached from one of its wires. The trapped streak of lightning broke free and leaped for Miss Wingbone in a line barbed with acute angles.

She saw the peasant for a moment like the negative of a photograph, with a black face and white eyes. She saw him no more. She gazed round. Her own room had disappeared. There was no door. She was well and truly in Waldo's room itself, the second citizen of Earth to enter the parallel universe of Sudonia.

Even now, the indefatigable girl stuck to her original theory.

'Good gracious,' she said, 'I have become a figment of Jonah's imagination.'

CHAPTER TWELVE

Miranda and her ladies were about to go indoors for the evening when the mob rushed past them again, not brandishing weapons or shouting slogans this time, but whimpering and babbling and casting fearful glances behind them.

'They are in exceeding haste,' she remarked.

'Do not venture near them, madam,' said the ladies nervously.

'Fiddlesticks, forsooth,' said Miranda, and walked some paces nearer to the human torrent, to discover that its babbling had one word in common, the word *witch* frenziedly repeated.

'Witch,' she said thoughtfully.

She suspected that Jonah must have a mistress, because he seemed so bored in her own company. A mistress of Jonah's would very likely be a witch.

Like the Lord Chamberlain before her, she had her doubts about Jonah's circumstances. She had kissed 'the tiger-coloured stone' at the suggestion of Mad Waldo, and then, lo and behold, her champion had arrived, looking like some relation of Waldo's, with a squire who looked very like Waldo himself. Waldo, she had heard, was never to be found in his hut these days . . .

Certainly Jonah had done all that had been expected

of him. His two feats of arms had been truly impressive. But they had been clever rather than courageous, and Miranda, being a true princess, kept cleverness firmly in its place. Jonah didn't behave like one of noble blood. He didn't understand court custom. Really, he would have been better off in some alchemist's cell, inventing miraculous things. It was all he was fit for.

Nevertheless he had won back all her father's lands and belongings for him, and without doubt she would have to marry him.

Miranda paced up and down considering the matter. Two courses were open to her: to elope with someone (but with whom?) or to marry Jonah and make the best of it (but how?). Her gaze fell on the figure of Hubert, who was lying on his side on the ground, propped up on one elbow, his cheek on his fist, his eyes beholding her with mournful yearning; and her spirit kindled. No, she did *not* consider granting Hubert his desires and becoming his mistress. That would spoil everything, especially for Hubert, because she realized that his mood of gentle melancholy was a most enjoyable state. She saw that, if things turned out as she expected, she too might be in a similar one. Miranda saw herself in prospect as a Sorrowful Queen. That were a delightfully romantic thing to be.

She went back slowly to her ladies. 'Woe is me,' she said experimentally.

'Alas, dearest child,' said the eldest of the ladies, 'how is't that woe is thee?'

'Well, actually,' said Miranda, who was the opposite of her father in that she would commit herself only to certainties, 'it would be more accurate to say that woe is probably me. It depends on how things turn out.' She smiled a small secret smile. 'A witch,' she murmured. 'I must seek out this witch.'

Miss Wingbone took stock of the situation. The peasant, like Jonah on the university slopes, had vanished completely. She contemplated the broken cone. Even if Waldo mended it, there would be no way back, for until now, at any rate, he had found no way of breaking through to her world. What was more, the mirror in her living room would surely be disturbed, sooner or later. People would come looking for her . . . She also speculated on what advance Towpath Ltd would make, with neither herself nor Jonah to oppose them, but that consideration seemed unreal, from here . . .

Unreal: no, *this* was unreal, this world to which she had come. The very name suggested it. How did one spell it? Pseudo-nia?

She was surprised how little dismay she felt. She was here with no possessions, not even a toothbrush, dressed as if for a ball (except for her shoes, which she had not bothered to change, and which were flat-heeled and black, with laces), but none of this seemed to matter. She accepted everything naturally, as if in a dream. She *was* in a dream, someone else's.

Better find him, she supposed, and say, look, I've got into your dream through no fault of my own. How about board and lodging and a change of clothes? And in all propriety you'd better introduce me to the princess, and explain my presence here.

Mind you, Miranda might not believe that story about the mirror. One could hardly blame her if she didn't . . .

All the same, said Miss Wingbone to herself, frowning, I got engaged to Jonah first. He can't talk about 'circumstances' any more. The circumstances are that I am here and here I shall probably have to stay, and I've got the first claim to him . . .

She began roaming through the palace. It was deserted; everyone was hiding in terror. Descending into a courtyard, she came upon a crumpled figure, covered with dust, lying on the flagstones. She knelt by him, getting the silver gown dusty, and took off his helmet, and pillowed his head in her lap.

Sir Topas groaned and opened one eye. The other eye he could not open; it was shut tight, and turning blue-black.

'The knaves were too many for me,' he mumbled through swollen lips.

'Hush now,' said Miss Wingbone, 'and be careful how you move.'

'I could not reach my trusty sword, withal.'

'Don't exert yourself.'

'An I had reached my sword, it would have been different.'

'Yes of course,' said Miss Wingbone soothingly. She was a compassionate person, especially towards the weaker sex, with its childish bravado and pathetic defencelessness before the realities of life. 'But you must not exert yourself.'

Sir Topas heaved himself up, to fall back in her lap with a groan, but he began talking eagerly and haltingly.

'Shouldn't have trusted mob. Those dogs have no discipline. Least thing scares them. The varlets panicked . . . broke ranks . . . Yet, sooth to say, that Sprockett Hasp caitiff is cunning . . . apt to unnerve the stoutest . . . he has a magic sword. What signifies, a Goddes-name, when you smite at it and it faileth to connect? He shoots arrows right off target, yet they hit the bull . . . Verily, it is witchcraft . . . Mob thought he'd sent a witch to them. Panicked. Understandable, yet a lily-livered lot, withal . . .'

But his good eye now took in just what it was looking at. It was the Witch who had panicked the mob.

'Harrow,' he said weakly, and sank back, shattered.

'Look,' said Miss Wingbone kindly but firmly, 'you must not get so excited and you must keep still. You may have broken some bones. It would be unwise to move you and anyway beyond my strength. You must lie here till I bring you help. I am going to look after you.' She lowered his head with extreme gentleness back to the flagstones, wincing as she did so, but there was nothing in sight to serve for a cushion. 'I'll be as quick as I can,' she said. 'There must be *someone* about.'

She took off her dark glasses and chewed the side-piece, looking at him ruminatively for a moment. For the second time that afternoon Sir Topas was stunned. He gazed up at her and spoke in deeply humble tones.

'I shall obey you, gentle adventurous lady.'

When the mob rushed into the palace, the servants and courtiers and even soldiers inside the building took a less languid view of them than did those outside. After one panic-stricken glance at the rioting forest of weapons, they dashed for cover, cowering in broom cupboards and under beds and even in dustbins. There they stayed, marvelling at the ominous hush that had fallen on the mob. When it went into reverse and charged out, they cautiously poked their noses out. As the tail of the rout went over the drawbridge, they grew bolder and came into the open. What was it those ruffians were babbling? Something about a witch! This heartened them. A witch! Ha ha! That could mean nothing else but a bit of bluff on the part of the brilliant Knight of the Sprockett Hasp, who could shoot arrows at right angles. A timely magic trick! They resumed their duties, laughing heartily.

But Jonah, hiding in the Lord Chamberlain's room,

did not know of his latest reputation. He thought he had been disgraced. Where had he been? they would ask. What kind of hero was he, to let a mob of peasants ransack the palace?

'If only they'd carried knives, or kept the axeheads on their picks, or studded their chair-legs with nails,' he lamented, 'my sword would have defeated them, but no one's yet learned how to magnetize wood.'

'They are too loutish for knightly combat,' agreed Waldo glumly. 'Against ignorance the gods themselves battle in vain.'

'Yet something scared them off,' said Jonah, when at last they crept out and picked their way through the corridors amidst a litter of discarded blunt instruments.

They regained Waldo's room without meeting a soul, and there the broken cone confronted them. Waldo sank to the floor in despair.

'Trapped for ever in Sudonia!'

'It's all very well for you, you live here. What about me?'

'You like it here.'

'I thought I did,' said Jonah, 'but . . .' He considered. 'I'm homesick! That's what I am!' The true nature of his situation dawned on him. 'Trapped! Yes, trapped! You must mend the cone! You've got to mend the cone!'

'Look,' said Waldo becoming calmly and sadly reasonable, 'suppose I do? What good will it do?'

'That's true,' said Jonah dully.

'You got here by accident through a freak thunderstorm.'

'Yes.'

'There's never been any hope of getting back.'

'I don't know,' said Jonah slowly. 'Miss Wingbone might come up with something.'

'She is very bright,' said Waldo uncertainly.

'Arguably the cleverest – '

'Yes. Well, we'll give her every chance. I'll set about mending the cone at once.'

'That's the spirit.'

'Mind you, trapping a streak of lightning isn't easy. Not a job for your average poacher.'

'No, of course not, old chap.'

'But with our combined brains – '

'That's the spirit.'

Together they worked the cone back into position and rewired it. It was dead, of course, being without its battery of lightning, but they were heartened even to do this much. They were looking at each other with mild satisfaction when there was a commotion in the corridor outside: yelps of fear, a scurry of footsteps, and one sharp cry of rage in a voice they recognized. They dashed into the corridor and met the voice's owner: it was Miss Wingbone, resplendent in a silver gown (but with singularly ill-matching shoes) and very angry.

'Oh, it's you. Just about time. Are all the people mad here?'

The people, quite simply, were scared out of their wits. Laughing happily at the thought of a witch that had frightened the simple peasants, they had come, in their various groups and couples, upon the witch herself, glittering in silver and with terrible gleaming black discs for eyes. Most of them ran; a few fell flat on their faces. The dreadful witch had cursed them in a voice rising to a shriek, flinging from group to group as if she would cast a horrible spell on the whole palace. She raged along corridors, up flights of stairs.

With no word of explanation for her presence she accosted Jonah and Waldo, still angry and exasperated.

'There's a man in a courtyard below who may be seriously injured. All I'm asking is for *someone* to help me move him to a bed. I can't carry a strecher by myself. Can't hold both ends at once. Do you think anyone will listen? All they do is run away. Well, please come on. There's no time to lose.'

But the two men had not recovered from the shock. 'Fair lady, by your leave –' began Waldo faintly.

'Waldo, this is no time for gadzookery. Nor,' added Miss Wingbone, as Jonah's hand went instinctively to his pocket, 'is it the time for crosswords!'

'But how did you get here?' demanded Jonah.

'Nor for long-winded explanations. Come on.'

Resignedly, they accompanied Miss Wingbone, watched from cover by dozens of pairs of fearful eyes. They improvised a stretcher from two pikes, taken from prostrate soldiers, and two coats, taken from the backs of stricken courtiers. With Waldo guiding, they carried Sir Topas up two flights of stairs to an unoccupied chamber opposite Jonah's suite, and laid him on the unmade bed.

'Now,' said Miss Wingbone, 'I shall require bed-clothes for this man, towels and bandages, and plenty of hot water. And, incidentally, a room of my own. It looks as if I may be staying here for quite a while.'

More than once, while all this was going on, Jonah had reached for his pocket, only to look lost, like a gunfighter who had mislaid his gun. He stared at Sir Topas, then at Miss Wingbone, and shook his head dazedly.

'I never imagined this would happen.'

'Actually you did, Jonah,' said Miss Wingbone. She looked closely at the groaning Sir Topas. 'I am afraid your imagination has become feverish.'

CHAPTER THIRTEEN

Miss Wingbone quickly got all the things she had asked for, with the added bonus of a plentiful change of clothes. She was accepted by everyone with extraordinary readiness. The king himself was particularly nice about her. 'See that she is attended with all courtesy while she remaineth,' he said, like the good old man he was. But was it not remarkable that no one challenged her presence in Sudonia, but treated it as if it were the most natural thing in the world?

Waldo had spun some yarn about her, of course. Even so . . .

And then it occurred to her that, if she were living in a dream, this attitude to her was quite in order. Everything is taken for granted in a dream.

What was more, things are left out of it; those everyday details that make waking life so pedestrian and so dull. She tried an experiment. She asked Jonah:

'Where is the queen?'

'What queen?' he replied, as if guiltily.

'*The* queen, Jonah. The king's wife. Miranda's mother.'

'I – I've never met her.'

Waldo explained that the queen was dead. But Miss Wingbone believed that she had never been alive, simply because Jonah had never thought of her. Yet now, within the hour, they came upon a huge portrait of her over the fireplace in the great entrance hall. Jonah was amazed that he had never seen it before. Miss Wingbone was not surprised in the least. Until this moment, it hadn't been there.

The queen was very like Miranda in the face, but she had three chins.

'Miranda in twenty years' time,' said Miss Wingbone, smiling.

Jonah nodded glumly. This was something he didn't care to think about. Miss Wingbone smiled more widely.

Even if she were living in a dream, however, she had to treat it as real while she was in it, and Sir Topas needed all her care. He was very strong physically, and was rapidly recovering from his injuries, but she was concerned about the state of his mind. He seemed to have lost all belief in himself. Seemed? He *had*. He had sustained two crushing defeats at the hands of people he despised, and he was humiliated.

Everyone treated him well. While he was a guest at the palace, knightly courtesy demanded it. Page-boys peeled grapes for him. The king sent minstrels to play to him. Miranda came in regularly with single roses, which Miss Wingbone arranged in vases all round the room. All this attention depressed him. He felt like an old war-horse put out to grass. He was not dangerous any more.

'Victim of magic,' he muttered, as he was wont to do, over and over again. 'No chance against magic.'

'Don't upset yourself,' said Miss Wingbone helplessly.

'That Lord Chamberlain upstart,' volunteered Sir Topas, 'he understood it.'

'Oh?' said Miss Wingbone, all attention.

'Yes. Heard him telling mob. Mystic formula. Magic words on paper. Some of them vertical – '

He continued rambling in this vein for some while, until she grasped what he was talking about.

'Crosswords! No magic about it. Mere reasoning. I'll show you how to do one.'

'You're a witch,' said Sir Topas hoarsely and fearfully. 'You'll put a spell on me.'

Miss Wingbone studied the simple-minded giant with sympathy. If she went about it carefully, she might find the very cure for his state of mind.

'It's a good spell. It strengthens the brain.'

'Could do with some of that,' muttered Sir Topas. He squinted at her apprehensively. 'You'd not deceive me? Not turn me into a toad, nothing like that?'

'Haven't I looked after you?'

'Ah, so you have.'

'Well, then.'

She made up an elementary crossword for him, using a quill pen and parchment supplied by Waldo. He was terribly suspicious at first, and kept looking at his hands to see whether webs were forming between his fingers, but with her infinitely patient encouragement he tackled it at last.

Bearing in mind the lines his mind ran on, she composed a puzzle of two clues, as follows:

Clues: Across 1. How to treat a dastardly foe (4,3,9)

Down 1. How to treat another dastardly foe (4,3,9)

He brooded over this for a long time, growling at the thought of a dastardly foe.

'Treat it naturally,' encouraged Miss Wingbone. 'What would you do to a dastardly foe?'

'Hack him manfully, withal.'

'Excellent! There's no need for the "withal", though.'

She had allowed for his mediaeval spelling. She watched him with something like maternal pride as, with his tongue sticking out, he laboriously wrote in 'hack hym manfullie' for one across.

'Now, what about one down? You can't repeat yourself, of course.'

His self-confidence greatly boosted, he looked at one down with a kindling eye.

'Hew him jauntily, forsooth.'

'Splendid! Of course, you must leave out the "forsooth".'

He beamed at her in a state of intellectual exultation, and wrote in 'Hewe hym jauntilie.'

'There!' said Miss Wingbone. 'We'll soon try using two clues across, and two down.'

'Getting rather profound, isn't it?'

'You'll be quite equal to it. You're a very quick learner.'

'You really think so? You know, this is cheering me up!'

Miss Wingbone was cheered up too. Sir Topas was bringing out qualities in her which she had only dimly known she possessed.

Or was it Sir Topas who was doing this? Was it in reality Jonah himself? If all that went on in Sudonia was only a projection of Jonah's secret wishes – as she herself still believed – could it be that she was playing a rôle that he unconsciously wanted her to play? Good Heavens. She produced a small hand mirror and studied herself in it. 'A ministering angel?' she demanded of herself. '*Thou*?'

Astonishingly, considering the unceremonious way she had been pitched into Sudonia, Miss Wingbone was happy. She was considering asking the king for a grant to build a hostel for battered knights in that peaceful valley where the unicorn lived. She thought less and less about returning to earth and Sprockett's Electricals. If this were a dream, let her go on dreaming. Miranda? She was not jealous of Miranda any more. The odds had lengthened on Miranda.

But Waldo was not happy. For one thing, his chances of entering Miss Wingbone's world seemed finally to have gone; but apart from that, he was jealous of her personally; he was a great genius, but she had a power that he lacked. It was the greatest force in the universe. He envied her.

Jonah was not happy either. He worried about not being happy. Hadn't he gone beyond the ends of the earth to find happiness? This made him unhappier still. He feared that he must be a born malcontent. He had preferred Cinderella to Miss Wingbone, then Miranda to Miss Wingbone, and then Miss Wingbone to Miranda; but now that Miss Wingbone was here, that didn't please him either. The grass was always greener on the other side . . . She was paying too much attention to that Topas fellow . . .

Would he be happy with her back at Sprockett's Electricals? If you thought about it, the question was absurd.

Nor was Miranda happy. Miss Wingbone made her feel inferior – her, a princess! When she called on Sir Topas, bearing single roses, Miss Wingbone did not curtsey; she did not even look round. 'Ah yes, thank you: just leave it on the table, will you? You must excuse us, we're going to have our bath.' Miranda knew that Miss Wingbone was a powerful sorceress, and you had to be careful with powerful sorceresses. But really! *We* are going to have our *bath*!!

She had supposed that the new witch would be Jonah's mistress, and this did not displease her, because it would relieve her of some of her obligations and pave her way to becoming a Sorrowful Queen. But it seemed that she'd got it wrong; the witch spent all her time with Sir Topas, and Sir Topas spent all his time gazing at the witch in much the same way as Hubert gazed upon herself; and although, when Sir Topas had won her in a wager, she had thought her fate to be worse than death, she did not at all like his new indifference to her. She bit her lip. Perhaps single roses were not enough, in the circumstances.

Sprockett's Electricals, with its many strata of executives, managers, and representatives, continued to function without Jonah and Miss Wingbone, much as a dance band will play on without its leader.

But the junior clerk, Peacock, missed Miss Wingbone badly. Having decided to worship her (therapeutically) he was aggrieved when she was absent.

Peacock liked to do everything in order. It is possible that his unconscious mind itself worked by clockwork. He had taken his job with Sprockett's Electricals to earn a wage, but systematically ignored his duties because he intended to become a writer. To this end he had committed to memory some impressive words: *ominous, sinister, foreboding, grim*. At present he tended to use them in a lump, but that was just inexperience. In the cause of his health, he kept to a strict diet (his starving, which had worried Miss Wingbone, was like Hubert's swoon, not to be taken literally) – and chewed every mouthful a hundred times, although he found counting – ninety-seven, ninety-eight, ninety-nine – rather tedious. When embracing his girl-friend, Sharon, he timed himself by glancing discreetly at his wristwatch.

Whenever he decided upon a course of action, he entered wholly into the spirit of it. Thus, although he deliberately picked on Miss Wingbone (without glasses) to idealize, he was quite genuinely infatuated with her. (By the same process, some arranged marriages can be completely successful, and happier than many formed by haphazard choice.) But in order for him to go on being infatuated, Miss Wingbone had to be there.

One of his duties, which he carried out thoroughly, because it involved her, was to sort out the post in the morning and take it round. The stacks of letters that he took into Miss Wingbone's room now began to resemble the Long Thing in bulk. They formed a column in her in-tray which toppled over and spread all over her desk, her chair and the floor. Peacock was at a loss where to put the latest batch. He opened the drawers of her desk with a mind to disposing of it there.

In doing so, he found something he recognized: a bunch of keys: her spare car keys and the spare Yale key to her flat.

His heart began beating fast.

A future writer, Peacock dramatized everything. He pictured Miss Wingbone dead in her flat. Or gagged and tied to a chair, perhaps – she was extremely wealthy and worth burgling. Golly, if she'd been tied to a chair for this long, three days, she'd probably be dead as well.

He worried about it all day. Suppose she was simply working at home? It would look awkward if he let himself in and ran into her, wouldn't it? When it was time to go home he went into her office and phoned her flat, listening to the ringing tone for fully five minutes before putting the phone down. When he reached the flat, he rang several times and called her name through the letter-box. Then he let himself in, shifting three milk bottles indoors and picking up some letters from the mat.

He was trembling all over. On the train he had composed scene after scene depicting his rescue of her, some of them ending with his getting the George Cross, but all involving her boundless gratitude and love. He intended to be faithful to Sharon, though. 'I just did what any decent person would have done,' he would say lightly. To each scene he added extra characters – police, doctors, ambulance men, nurses, newspaper reporters – but he was the hero in all of them.

The flat was empty. In the living room he came upon Jonah's mirror, dead centre, and facing the windows. The glass was angled slightly away from the frame and wedged with a clothes peg. It fascinated him, perhaps because he associated it with Miss Wingbone. He removed the clothes peg and began turning the little wheel on the frame, watching himself in the mirror all the while. Suddenly his image in the mirror disappeared.

He looked down at himself in alarm. He could see himself all right. He ranged through the flat, found a long mirror on the bedroom wall, and was shocked to discover that it, too, held no reflection of him, though he paced before it and struck attitudes from every angle. He stumbled panic-stricken back to Jonah's mirror and began feverishly to turn the wheel. Once or twice his image flashed across the glass, raising his hopes, but he lacked Jonah's delicacy of touch. He swung the wheel wildly round, and made himself disappear completely, even to himself.

Finally, there being nothing else for it, he went home, in consternation and despair. His parents were greatly concerned about his disappearance. That is meant quite literally; they did not suppose that he was missing, for he spoke to them in a high-pitched voice and made things seem to float in the air.

CHAPTER FOURTEEN

Sir Topas's injuries being nearly healed, he was able to leave his bed and lie on a couch, where he solved crossword puzzles all day long. They had become his obsession and his delight, but a source of worry, too, like all serious games. He was quick to solve clues involving sword-play, but all other subjects – flowers, fish, fountains, girls and guitars, romance and roses – had him groping and all but lost. Miss Wingbone, having composed the puzzles, helped him, but she knew that to solve them himself would do him the greatest good, and so she began to leave him alone for longer periods.

Miranda took note of her absence, and one afternoon, just after Miss Wingbone had left, she went quietly up to Sir Topas's room.

He was greatly changed in his manner. Instead of ogling her, his sensual lips curling from his strong white teeth in a leer, he looked at her mildly and absently, while continuing to employ his strong white teeth in chewing the end of a pen. 'Pray do not rise, Sir Knight,' said Miranda, but he plainly had no intention of doing so. She stuck the rose she had brought him into a vase and sat on the edge of his bed.

'What labour is this that so engrosses you, sir?'

'It's a crossword.'

'And what, pray, may that be, witchcraft?'

'No, it exercises ye reasoning faculties.'

'What merit is in that?' asked Miranda coldly. 'As we already know what we have need to know, what cause have we to reason about it?'

'It is pleasant sport, for the nones.'

'The sorceress hath taught it you.'

'No sorceress, madam, but a saintly woman with a rare gift of healing.'

'You are inconstant, Sir Topas,' said Miranda, and she frowned severely, but in her heart there was a twinge of dismay. 'Truly are you called False. But a little while ago you felt such ardour for me that you saw fit to abduct me, and now you transfer your affections to this emaciated creature.'

'Inconstant?' echoed Sir Topas. 'Inconstant. Oh, no. Nothing like that. Don't think of her in that way, not at all.'

'That is as well, sir,' said Miranda, slightly mollified, but still cold. 'Anyone who embraced her would be in danger of cutting himself to pieces.'

Sir Topas was finding this conversation embarrassing, and he did, unwittingly, what Jonah would have done in the circumstances.

'What a soldier wears, seven letters?' he enquired. 'It begins with "u".'

'I have no idea.'

'One across reads, "animal with one horn", seven letters,' went on Sir Topas fretfully. 'I have put "unicorn". Surely that must be right? Thus, one down must begin with "u". But: "What a soldier wears"? Sword? Helmet? Buckler? These do not fit.'

Reluctantly, Miranda approached the couch and studied the puzzle.

' "Uniform",' she suggested begrudgingly.

'You have hit it!' exclaimed Sir Topas, so warmly that she could not help feeling pleased. 'So: four across begins with "f". "Fit to be hewn jauntilie", three letters. Ha, that will be "foe". Let us see: three down. "Frozen water", three letters.'

'Ice,' said Miranda, with a slight kindling of interest.

'That word was eke on the tip of my tongue,' said Sir Topas triumphantly. 'But what of eight across? "Manner in which dastardly foe should be hacked", nine letters. I think I have this. How think you?'

'Manfullie?' suggested Miranda timidly.

'Gracious madam, you have a natural gift for this!'

'Just a bit of jolly good luck, actually,' said Miranda, flushing with pleasure.

'You are over-modest.'

'This is a merry sport, Sir Knight!'

Certainly it made a change from dancing in a ring and listening to very long poems. She sat beside Sir Topas and began to peruse the puzzle in earnest. When Miss Wingbone returned they were perched close together on the couch like placid love-birds, their two minds engrossed in the same pursuit. A new dimension had been added to their lives.

Peacock's invisibility soon became international news. When he changed into clothes that had not been affected his outline became visible again, and when a hat, dark glasses, and a beautifully modelled face mask were added, he looked something of an improvement on his original self, but he often reverted to invisibility to avoid publicity. He had the advantage over other pestered celebrities in that he could disappear almost at will. Photographers could not take pictures of nothing.

He was interviewed in numerous TV bulletins and

chat shows, and drew protests from thousands of viewers that trick photography was being used, but when everyone was satisfied that his state was genuine, offers involving huge sums of money came flooding in. The Secret Service was particularly interested, because he would make an ideal spy, but there were many propositions from business houses, too, and several from terrorist organizations. The one thing they had in common was the desire to destroy.

Peacock made a small fortune without giving anything away, except that his condition was the outcome of an invention of Jonah Sprockett's. He declared that it had happened by accident and that he hadn't a clue how it was done, which was true, of course.

He studiously made no mention of the mirror, and he turned down every offer of a job. This was very wise of him. He had made up his mind to become a writer, and he could see that with a small fortune and no need to do other work he would be able to devote himself to this calling, whereas with a large fortune and a lot of obligations he would never have a minute to himself. But the mirror still fascinated him. He revisited Miss Wingbone's flat regularly. He would change into his invisible clothes at home and then go boldly up to her door with no fear of detection, and spend long periods staring into the mirror. But he never touched the wheel, for fear of making himself visible again. He was strongly tempted to do so, however, as one is tempted to dab a finger on wet paint.

Meanwhile, shares in Sprockett's Electricals shot up, and the takeover attempts of Towpath Ltd became hopeless. Towpath's managing director, having lost thirty-five million pounds on publicity during the unsuccessful campaign, resigned, and took to sailing round the world in his yacht, to the great benefit of his health.

Miss Wingbone came away from Sir Topas's room feeling well pleased, but she hadn't gone far before doubts set in. What was in it for *her*?

Her rôle in life seemed to be to get down with a spanner to people's problems, leaving them free to love others. Sir Topas was the latest in the line. He admired her, he worshipped her, even, but she was too clever for him, and so he gave his love to someone else. Everyone seemed to do the same.

Diffidently, she tackled Jonah.

'Your bride-to-be is taking a lot of interest in Sir Topas.'

'Oh, good.'

'Good?'

'Yes. This engagement has been worrying me. They'd keep wanting me to do heroic things. I should find that depressing.'

'Everything depresses you, Jonah.'

'I know. Depressing, isn't it?'

'If ever we get back to earth, will you still want to marry me?'

'Oh yes.'

'Come, that's promising.'

'Well, if I married you, I could forget all about romance and being in love and all that nonsense. It is superficially exciting, but in the end it causes depression.'

'I suppose as an alternative you could simply open a vein and bleed to death.'

Alone in her room again, Miss Wingbone looked at herself in her mirror and remarked, 'What an attractive prospect faces me in either world!' She took off her spectacles and fairly gnawed the side-piece. 'But I ask for it. I'm too clever and not clever enough. I could easily have outdone that little floosie in the pantomime, and Miranda too, if I'd put my mind to it. But then why should I? Go through life pretending to be stupid?' She grinned at her reflection. 'I should find that depressing!'

She sought out Waldo. He spent all his time in his room nowadays, the hermit of the wood all over again. She was sorry for him, because she was sure that he was building his hopes in vain.

He was seated before the cone. He greeted her as he always did, looking round briefly with a mad gleam in his blue eyes.

'Not yet!'

'Waldo, I must talk to you.'

She sat opposite him and very earnestly outlined the theory that had dominated her for so long. 'Jonah is a genius,' she said, 'and like other geniuses before him, he has brought off a miracle by a fluke. That mirror of his turns dreams into reality. Sudonia is his dream. It's a singularly muddled one, the people don't even know what century they're in, but dreams aren't logical. It is the greatest invention in the history of the world. But you see what it means, Waldo. You don't really exist.'

'I don't exist,' repeated Waldo mildly, and appeared to consider this with detached intellectual curiosity.

'Only in the mind of Jonah.'

'He dreamed up everything? Didn't I invent the cone?'

'You did, but he dreamed you inventing it.'

'So what this amounts to is that you and he could enter your world, but I never can?'

'I'm afraid so, Waldo. You see, Jonah has made a dream-world real, but it's only real so long as he stays in it. Do you follow me?' Waldo nodded, but he was watching her like a chess player who sees his opponent moving a piece towards defeat. 'You see, Waldo, to try to get you into our world would be like trying to fish the reflection of the moon out of a pool. It's only there so long as it stays there.'

'Very nicely put.'

'Oh, Waldo, I'm sorry to tell you you don't exist, it sounds so – so *dismissive* – and you're so extraordinarily clever, too – '

'Yes, much cleverer than Jonah.'

'But of course you are, Waldo, because you are what he would like himself to be.'

'In that case, imaginary though I am, I should be able to help him.' So far from being put out, Waldo was bubbling with secret glee. To Miss Wingbone's astonishment, he seized her hand and kissed it. 'Why haven't I thought of this before? You have inspired me. You are a wonderful woman. I owe you so much.'

'Join the group,' said Miss Wingbone sadly. 'But what will you help him to do?'

'Dream up a thunderstorm.'

'So that you can trap the lightning again? But that would only get you back to where you started. After that you'd need another accident, like the peasant knocking over the cone.'

'If your theory is right, Jonah must have dreamed that too, so perhaps I can make him dream it again.'

'But even if you did, it would have to work in reverse to get us back to earth!'

'Perhaps I'll have to make him dream in reverse.'

'But even if you do . . .' Miss Wingbone shook her head and gave up. 'Waldo, you're an optimist.'

'No, better than that. I'm mad.'

During the next few days Waldo stayed locked in his room, concentrating so intensely that he gave off vibrations, causing a shimmer in his vicinity like a heat haze.

In normal times he would have been missed, seemingly neglecting his duties as Jonah's squire, but times were not normal. The princess was so taken with the new game that she paid no attention to court routine. Sir Topas was now able to leave his couch and limp about, and Miranda and her ladies would sit with him in a circle in their field doing crossword puzzles. Each would make up her own, which the others would copy out, and then twist themselves into agonized contortions as they wrestled with the clues.

Jonah was in lower spirits than ever. The crosswords were growing fast in sophistication, and the clues were often beyond his wits, and after some frustrated attempts he refused to play any more. The weather was getting him down, too; it had become unbearably sultry. Such drowsy heaviness hung upon him that he could scarcely breathe.

'I wish this storm would break,' he kept repeating.

CHAPTER FIFTEEN

The atmosphere in Sudonia was stifling. Miss Wingbone thought that Waldo was brewing the impending storm simply by brooding on it, but if the storm were imaginary, it was giving everybody an imaginary headache.

Miranda's ladies were particularly upset. They had been brought up to believe that thought was harmful to women, leading to an intellectual look that spoiled their beauty, and they were troubled by fears about the new craze, as though they had succumbed to some drug with side effects; but so strong was it that they couldn't give it up, and furtively discussed clues with one another in corners.

The storm came without rain. The thunder barked and crackled and the lightning flared in hellish spasms. All Sudonia crouched under its anger. Jonah and Miss Wingbone took refuge in Waldo's room, round which he was scampering like a white mouse on its wheel, continually adjusting the mirrors on the walls. He paused momentarily to seize Miss Wingbone's hand and kiss it, then went on jumping about, giggling to himself.

They made to sit down, the better to observe Waldo's undignified behaviour, but wherever they sat he shooed them off. Resignedly, they chose a mirror-free corner, and sat with their feet sticking out, Miss Wingbone in a cream-coloured gown patterned with pink roses, and Jonah in a silver-grey doublet, the sleeves slashed with scarlet. Waldo was hysterical, and deserved having been called mad. Yet something was happening, or trying to happen, for more than once the mirrors were lanced with narrow bands of sizzling white light, such as Miss Wingbone had seen when she had first tried to operate Jonah's mirror in her living room. Each time, Waldo gave an expectant cry, only to follow it with a snarl of disappointment. At last he sagged on to a chair, all fury spent.

'It's no good.'

The next flash of lightning was weak, a mere blink, and the thunder that lazily followed sounded farther away.

'I'm beaten.'

Miss Wingbone stood up, dusted herself, and put her arm round Waldo's bowed and shaking shoulders. She was deeply sorry for him, not only on account of this failure, but for the whole gamut of his impossible hopes and ambitions. Jonah, sitting on his heels, looked at her curiously. It had never occurred to him that she was capable of tenderness. Of looking after people's needs, yes. Sprockett's Electricals had the best welfare department in the business world. But tender? – about as much as a clinical thermometer, he would have said. He was quite touched. He stood up, intending to give Waldo a consoling pat on his own account.

But at that very moment Waldo sprang off his chair with a strangled cry, and grabbing Miss Wingbone, flung her to the floor, dropping down beside her. A weak, positively bland flash of lightning seemed to have got caught up in one of the mirrors, which glowed like the discreet lighting in a furniture store; and then it hopped round the walls, making the room like a revolving lantern. For a stunned moment the room was dark. When their eyes were adjusted to normal daylight again, they saw that the cone was revolving as of yore, the lightning trapped inside it swirling and glinting as it spiralled endlessly into its tip.

A hush fell on Sudonia, broken only by a sweet tinkle of music from the birds. The unicorn made its appearance in dainty little trips to the opal pool. In the mellow afterglow of the storm, the landscape looked once again as it had appeared to Jonah on that first evening when he had seen it from his flat. No one would have suspected that there were worms and wodwos and robber bands in the woods, or disgruntled peasants in the outback. Although he was viewing the scene from the palace, on the side opposite to where he had been at first, everything, to his eyes, was in its original position, as if left and right had changed places; or as if, indeed, he were seeing it in a mirror.

But one detail was missing. No golden girl came out of the bushes. No golden girl showed up anywhere, for Miranda had gone, and so had all her ladies, and so had Sir Topas.

Soon the news came through that she had eloped with him to one of the mansions on his estate, where they planned to open a college for students of crosswords, with her ladies as the instructresses.

In a lengthy communication to her father, Miranda described the profound change that had come over Sir Topas. He was no longer False; in fact he never had been, only Misunderstood. The refined influence of gentlewomen, plus the mental stimulus of solving crosswords, had transformed his nature, so that he no longer desired to hack and hew dastardly foes, but declared that he loved everybody, including even the mob, for whose benefit he proposed to found a number of schools.

From the brisk businesslike tone of her letter, it was plain that a change had come over Miranda too. She was no longer content to dally with Hubert and his kind, and play at being a Sorrowful Queen. She was charged with the zeal of social reform. You imagined her addressing meetings and distributing leaflets. Although he had been growing more and more uneasy at the thought of marrying her, this change in Miranda made Jonah quite desolate.

The king took his daughter's elopement extremely well. He was impressed by what Miranda told him about Sir Topas's business ability. Before his reform he had used this to swindle people who betted with him, but now he was going to turn it all into promoting Topas, Ltd. Crosswords were going to be a growth industry in Sudonia, and the king, in honour of his great office (and because his name would look good on prospectuses) would be a principal shareholder. Bevis was a sentimental man and was moved that his daughter had thought the kingdom well lost for love, while he himself thought a daughter well lost for so capital an investment.

So Miss Wingbone no longer had anyone to nurse and Jonah had no one to pay court to. They began to feel intrusive, in the bland atmosphere of Sudonia, as socially-minded flies might who had got into some ointment. The benevolent king gave orders: 'Let them be treated with all courtesy till they depart'; but he had no idea how difficult that would be for them.

Miss Wingbone rose from a good meal of roast swan and walked into the palace grounds, now all but deserted since Miranda had left. There she came upon the courtier Hubert, sitting on a daisied bank with his head in his hands, the picture of woe. Touched by unhappiness as she always was, she took off her spectacles and hesitatingly chewed the side-piece, uncertain whether to speak to him or not. She was wearing her cream gown with the pink roses, and her golden hair rippled about her shoulders. Hubert looked up, and fell down in a swoon.

Immediately, like a chorus in a ballet prancing on stage on cue, his followers surrounded him, raised him up, and forced wine between his pallid lips. He looked up at them with languishing eyes, and said faintly:

'Take me unto that lady, for sooth to say, I am half dead for love of her.'

Miss Wingbone replaced her spectacles.

'Congratulations, Hubert,' she said, 'and long may you live to enjoy it.' And she walked away, all sympathy spent.

'But, Jonah, if I understood you rightly, losing Miranda was exactly what you wanted.'

'You're too logical.'

'Am I? It comes of being a woman, I suppose.'

'All right, I may have said something in an offhand way about wanting rid of her, but now she's gone I feel terrible.'

Miss Wingbone studied him dispassionately. 'There is no cure for your disease,' she said.

'No, no. Lonely to my grave, I expect.'

Miss Wingbone did, however, still feel sorry for Waldo. His days as 'Jonah's squire' were numbered, because

Jonah would obviously have to leave the court eventually (and for where?) – and then Waldo would have to take off his black wig and go back to that wretched hut in the woods. If Jonah did by some miracle get back to earth, Waldo would cease to exist altogether. Either way, his prospects were uninviting.

Nevertheless he laboured on, never leaving his room, encouraged by some blips and squiggles of light in his mirrors in the evenings, and by an occasional faint shadowing of the end wall, as if the famous door were about to open and disclose Miss Wingbone's living room. She attributed these to general atmospherics, or possibly to Waldo's amazing personal vibrations, but he would not hear such negative talk.

Miss Wingbone was mistaken. The blips, squiggles and shadowings were caused in fact by Peacock, who let himself into the flat every evening. He did not tamper with the mirror, but struck various postures in front of it, like a demented Narcissus, simply to reassure himself that he was not reflected in it. He was invisible, and of course he could not carry his 'visible' clothing through the streets without arousing comment, but he overcame this, when he reached Miss Wingbone's flat, by wrapping himself in a crocheted bedspread from her bed. It enveloped him from neck to foot, so that he looked like a headless ghost.

When Waldo succeeded in retrapping the lightning, contact was set up between the cone and the mirror, although they were badly out of focus. Peacock's antics were affecting this, and once or twice he got a flicker of response from the mirror. Once, indeed, he even saw the reflection of himself wrapped in the bedspread, but extremely narrowed and elongated, as a figure on a court playing-card might see himself if he looked at the edge of it.

He was worried. He much enjoyed being invisible, and looked forward to a lifetime of the tranquillity that it brought. He prowled to and fro before the mirror: he crouched down and edged his way across it like a sheepdog watching its flock. He flapped his bedspread at it. After that one brief glimpse, there was no response, which was what he wanted, of course; but he could not resist testing it, in the way that one will keep poking a tongue against a suspect tooth.

Ah! There it was again! Peacock edgeways! He moved, and the narrow line of compressed bedspread vanished. But, as disturbed now as a householder who is convinced that he has heard a burglar, Peacock could no longer keep himself from touching the mirror itself, and with trembling (but invisible) fingers he reached out and turned the little wheel ever so slightly.

It chanced that this slight move was just what was needed to bring the mirror and Waldo's cone into exact contact. Peacock, staring into the mirror, became aware of a darkening of the room. He turned, and saw that the windows had been replaced by a black wall in which a door was outlined by four lines of light. Hugging the bedspread tightly round him, he crept towards it, and it opened by degrees, until it was almost wide.

Peacock hesitated, shaking and terrified. This must be an illusion. Miss Wingbone's flat was on the top floor. Supposing he were lured to walk right through her windows and go crashing to the street below? He hovered for a terrible moment. Then he heard voices, excitedly raised, and one of them was Miss Wingbone's.

This might be a delusion, but the voice of his idol summoned him like a siren. To give himself extra stability, he went down on all fours, wrapping the spare bit of bedspread over his head, and crept to the very threshold of the door. From there he saw a room whose walls were many-faceted with flashing mirrors, and in whose centre a cone, pearly with light, revolved; and behind the cone, a strawhaired man with madman's eyes; and on either side of him Mr Sprockett, wearing fancy dress, and Miss Wingbone, radiant in a gown all silver-white.

Miss Wingbone cried out again.

'There! There it is again! Look!'

Look they did; they stared; they blanched as white as her dress, for the object before their eyes was grotesque: a shapeless white mass some three feet high that flapped and grovelled. Most dreadful of all, it had no face, but a hollow cavity at the back of which a patch of its loathsome shroud could be seen.

'It's a Thing,' gasped Jonah. 'Waldo, this is some of your filthy magic!'

'It's an Elemental,' said Waldo, in sepulchral tones.

Miss Wingbone had now recovered. 'Whatever it is,' she said, 'it's wearing my bedspread.'

At which the Thing cried out, 'Oh Miss Wingbone, I can explain everything!'

'It's gibbering at us,' muttered Jonah.

'It's gibbering in Peacock's voice,' said Miss Wingbone, with gathering confidence.

The Thing stood up, and became a headless spectre.

'Miss Wingbone, I can ex – '

'I think you'd better. What are you doing in my flat, and why are you swathed in my bedspread?'

'About – about the – bedspread, Miss Wingbone, you see – I'm invisible.'

'That, Peacock, makes seeing rather difficult. Please tell me everything, beginning at the beginning.'

'Miss Wingbone, I was worried about you, you'd been missing for so long.' Peacock drew a breath. He knew that he had astounding news to impart, and he recovered his poise and rose to the occasion. 'Your absence seemed to me ominous, grim, foreboding, and sinister.'

'For Heaven's sake, boy, forget your literary pretensions and tell me the plain facts.'

Peacock lost his assurance again and falteringly did so, with promptings from Miss Wingbone that grew kinder as he went on, because he seemed so guilty and so upset. Besides, however much he had erred, he was their only contact with the earth, and required gentle handling.

'I've stopped the milk and newspapers for you, Miss Wingbone,' he concluded pathetically.

'Very thoughtful. Well. So you've become something of a celebrity? Sprockett's Electricals is in chaos, I suppose?'

'Oh no, Miss Wingbone. Everyone thinks you and Mr Sprockett are still around, invisible, and sort of – well, spying on them, and everyone's working like mad. They won't even stop for tea-breaks. I've given my notice, but I'm still there, and business is pouring in.'

'Much good may that do us.'

'You've only got to come back and see for yourself, Miss Wingbone.'

'Only,' said Miss Wingbone.

She walked slowly up to the doorway and reached out.

'Peacock, take my hand.'

The bedspread went into convulsions.

'Come along, take my hand.'

'I – I can't. I sort of . . . can't keep it steady.'

'Exactly. Now listen. On no account touch the mirror again. Leave it just as it is. Come back at this time every evening. Mr Waldo here will put you in touch by pressing this button. Peacock, I can't explain everything now, you couldn't stand it, but you must keep in touch with us. It may be no use, but it's our only hope.

'In the cupboard under the dresser in the kitchen you will find a round tin with a picture of a lady in a crinoline on it. Inside you will find a Christmas cake. Cut yourself a large slice. Mr Waldo will ring off now, Peacock. Be careful crossing roads.'

Waldo pressed the button, and his fantastic room and its occupants were replaced by Miss Wingbone's windows. The bedspread folded itself up neatly in the air, glided into a bedroom, and spread itself over a bed. In the kitchen a tin opened and a bread-knife cut a piece of cake, out of which semi-circles were chopped until it disappeared. The front door opened and shut itself. Phantom footsteps sounded on the stairs.

Every evening, Peacock kept his appointment with his employers. Instead of the bedspread, he now wore, at Miss Wingbone's suggestion, a loose-fitting overall from the broom cupboard, and faced them headless and legless, with gesticulating sleeves.

He would read them the share prices from *The Times*. Sometimes he read out the crossword clues. They would listen politely but showed no real interest.

Waldo was consumed by a single passion, to leave Sudonia for that other world. Sometimes he bubbled with optimism; sometimes he lapsed into gloom. For most of the day he sat before the cone, waiting for the time of Peacock's visit, and watching the cone turning, turning, turning. 'Dream in reverse,' he muttered, over and over again.

Jonah had decided that the whole of creation was a hollow sham. He wished to leave Sudonia, which hung in a trance now, like the Sleeping Beauty's bedchamber;

yet he did not particularly wish to go anywhere else. Both universes dissatisfied him. He was living in a sort of limbo.

Miss Wingbone felt protective towards Jonah, but he exasperated her too. Something was lacking in him. He had such a gift for being miserable everywhere that to return to earth, if that were possible, seemed pointless. As for Waldo, she dreaded his succeeding. To vanish like a bubble at the very moment of his success would be so cruel.

Yet she wanted to leave Sudonia too, for this country, always vague, as befitted a dream, had now become nebulous. It was like a landscape seen through mist. Where *was* everybody? Oh, they were there, the king, the lords and ladies who had thronged the tournaments, and the servants, and the common folk outside the grounds; they came and they went, and meals were provided, and beds were aired; but they were now all bit-players, as it were; and the only place that felt alive was the tiny focal point of Waldo's room, where the mad magician brooded all day, waiting for Peacock to flap the sleeves of the overall at him.

Then one evening the overall, in addition to flapping its sleeves, began to ripple, as if it were fluttering on a clothes-line.

'Keep still, Peacock,' snapped Jonah.

'I am keeping still, sir. It's you who are waving about. Sort of shimmying, sir.'

'You haven't touched the mirror, have you?'

'No, sir!'

'Vibrations,' muttered Jonah. 'From the street or somewhere. The adjustment's very delicate. Listen carefully, Peacock – '

And he told him how to fix the mirror's position with a clothes peg, as he had once before told Miss Wingbone.

This Peacock conscientiously did.

After this they all ran out of conversation. The overall assumed a self-conscious attitude.

Miss Wingbone, to break the silence, said:

'Funny, to fix such an advanced mechanism in such a simple way!'

This lame remark, which hardly merited an answer, galvanized Waldo. He sprang to his feet, remained rigid for a few moments, then rushed at Miss Wingbone and kissed her hand rapturously again and again.

'Yes, yes!' he cried. 'Oh, yes!'

Miss Wingbone had already found that she liked being kissed, even if it were only up to the wrist, but she was taken aback by the ardour of his response.

'Well, I'm so glad you agree –'

'Simplicity,' babbled Waldo. He really was, she decided, quite mad. 'Dear lady! You are so right. You always are so right. You have the gift to see through all our subtleties!' He seized her hand again and all but bit it. 'Simple! Ah, yes! You have it!'

'Oh, good.'

'So what simple thing are you going to do?' asked Jonah sardonically. 'Smash the cone with a hammer?'

Waldo shook him frenziedly by the hand. 'Dear friend! So you have understood!'

'He's raving,' said Jonah quietly. 'Humour him.'

'Better not let him get at a hammer, though.'

But Waldo had now simmered down into a state of delighted giggling.

'Care and method! That's the way!'

'They move slowly in Sudonia,' remarked Jonah. 'But how do you smash things with a hammer carefully and methodically?'

'Jonah,' said Miss Wingbone, torn between excitement and trepidation, 'I think he's on to something.'

Waldo began fashioning a sort of turntable, a flat, thick disc of wood with three handles sticking out of its edge. He cut a circle out of the middle, sawed the whole contraption in half, and then fitted the two halves round the base of the cone, fixing them with some powerful adhesive of his own making. Jonah was so taken with his skill that he tried to help him, but he could do nothing more expert than hold the tools, for Waldo was completely in command. Now the turntable was circling round with the cone, and much more rapidly than the leisurely spiralling of the lightning inside it would have led one to expect. Twenty protruding handles seemed to flash round its edge.

'Excellent,' said Waldo, stepping back to admire it.

'Er – ' said the overall from Miss Wingbone's room.

All three of them had forgotten Peacock, who had been standing there for hours.

'Ah yes, my boy. We shan't require you any longer tonight,' said Waldo. 'But be here tomorrow without fail.'

'Yes, sir,' said Peacock resignedly. Miss Wingbone felt sorry for him.

'How's Sharon taking all this, Peacock?'

'She says she doesn't see enough of me.'

Poor Peacock, Sharon literally saw nothing of him, and it was their fault.

'Tell her that if we get back I'll buy her a nice house for you both and furnish it,' said Miss Wingbone. 'It shall have a fridge, a freezer, a washing machine, and a colour TV. Goodnight, Peacock.'

Waldo pressed the button and Peacock vanished. The cone and its new attachment went turning on.

All the next day Waldo sat before the cone, never taking his eyes from it. Jonah and Miss Wingbone, having nothing else to do, did likewise, although to watch the blurred revolution of the turntable and its handles became sickening, as does watching the idiotic repetitions of a mechanical mannikin in a shop window. Waldo made it worse by refusing to discuss his plan with them. He was like some little boy in school with a secret. But at last the evening came. So presumably did Peacock; but Waldo did not press the button to contact him.

'Not yet. Stand by.'

'What for?'

'We're going to grab the handles and push against the motion of the cone.'

They looked at the handles, multiplied in a blur of speed.

'Impossible. We'd break our wrists.'

'Ah,' chanted Waldo, who was going mad again, 'but will you dare to follow if Waldo leads the way?' And darting forward, he made a lightning grab with his bony hands, and succeeded in clutching one of the handles. The cone continued turning; he was spun off his feet and dragged remorselessly round the table, his long body wiping the floor like a bolster. Kicking and straining, he managed to half-straighten himself, and, fighting with all his strength against the cone, slightly slowed it down.

'*Now*. Grab them.'

Hypnotized by his madness, they did so, shoving with all their might. The cone resisted them grimly. There was a rightness about its clockwise movement, so that to try to make it turn the other way seemed like defying the laws of nature. Nevertheless their combined and agonized wrestling slowed it down to a stop, so that neither it nor they could move.

Miss Wingbone's hair was blowing about her face like

Julie's in one of her typing frenzies. Her back ached and her hands were stuck to the handle. Her long skirt swished in the dust.

'Waldo,' she panted, 'just what the hell are we doing?'

Waldo replied, 'On the word three, heave. One, two, three, *heave!*'

So heave they did, and the cone, noiselessly, but with a strange shiver of protest, began to turn anti-clockwise, very slowly at first. It then gave a startling lurch, and all three, losing their grip, were pitched on to their hands and knees. The cone continued turning anti-clockwise in an aura of awful wrongness, and the lightning inside it, instead of spiralling to a point, now widened as it rose, each revolution opening it like a fan.

'Simplicity,' chortled Waldo breathlessly, 'and force of the human will. It can move mountains.'

'Waldo,' said Miss Wingbone, with patience that seemed ominously near hysteria, 'just what have we done? Have we changed the motion of the stars, anything like that? Will the sun now rise in the west and set east-by-north-east?'

'Not necessarily, but that is an interesting question,' replied Waldo civilly. 'Well, now – '

But Jonah, who had been tenderly massaging his aching forearms, exclaimed, 'I think I've gone left-handed!'

'Really?' said Waldo. 'Yes, there may be some slight side effects. Now, will you press the button, old chap?'

Grumbling, Jonah did so, using his left hand. The end wall darkened and the familiar door appeared. But it was now hung the opposite way. Its hinge-side, which had been on the right, was now on the left. It opened slowly as the overall that enwrapped Peacock approached it. The pocket on the overall, which had been on the left breast, was now on the right.

'Gnineve doog,' said the overall politely.

'Peacock,' remonstrated Miss Wingbone, 'this is not the time to practise your Lithuanian.'

'He's not. He's just said "good evening" backwards,' said Waldo. 'Don't speak to him, because you're speaking backwards too, and you'll confuse him.' And certainly Peacock, as far as a headless, handless and legless figure can manage it, did appear to be non-plussed. 'Now,' said Waldo, 'step right forward, please, and then stand perfectly still.' And even as they complied with this command, he produced a hammer from nowhere, and with one tremendous blow smashed the cone to pieces.

Only those who have been fired from the mouth of a cannon, or have ridden hobo-fashion on the outside of a space rocket, can imagine the sensation that was now experienced by Jonah and Miss Wingbone. They seemed to be spinning in the sky in the midst of a giant firework display. Morning-night, morning-night, dawn-sunset, dawn-sunset, sun-moon-stars, flashed the vision. Yet it is a most interesting scientific fact that when, as Waldo had planned, they came down to earth, on Miss Wingbone's deep-pile carpet, the clocks on the earth had moved forward only a few seconds. They had moved from imagination to fact, from dream to reality, and dreams, of course, can last only a few seconds, while seeming to span a period of months or even years. Science might explain this, but would probably get it wrong.

Miss Wingbone, who was wearing a silken gown of midnight blue, was the first to recover. Jonah was conscious but dazed. Peacock was visible again. He took off the overall sheepishly and stood there in his ordinary weekday suit.

He said anxiously, 'Miss Wingbone, are you all right?'

'I think so.'

'Mr Sprockett?'

'I think so. Give him time.'

'What about the other gentleman?'

'Oh no, no,' said Miss Wingbone, and tears came to her eyes. 'Mr Waldo is no more, I'm afraid.'

'But he was here a moment ago!'

'Yes, you saw him a moment ago, but that was in another country, and besides . . .' Miss Wingbone stopped suddenly. 'Here? You're sure? *Here*?'

'Yes, Miss Wingbone.'

In a wild surmise, she ranged through her flat, looking everywhere, in cupboards, under beds. She went on to the landing outside and looked in the lift. She opened her living room windows and stared into the street.

She turned back.

'No. It must have been a trick of the light.'

CHAPTER SIXTEEN

Miss Wingbone led Jonah discreetly to her car (he was wearing a crimson doublet sewn over with tiny pearls) and drove him home. In all his bizarre changes of costume, he had remembered to pocket his keys, so he was able to let himself in. He did not say a single word, but he did not seem depressed. On the contrary, he seemed to be brimming with peculiar elation, like an egg about to hatch.

Peacock came too, carrying the mirror. The glass was unbroken. The frame had been smashed, once again, by the recent shock. Well, let Jonah mend it, if he felt so inclined. She couldn't bear the sight of it any longer. Never again would she reassemble it.

'Never again,' she said to herself, alone at home. 'No, never again,' and by repeating these words over and over she made herself cry, a rare thing with her. She felt that she had literally lost a world, and not for love, either. For what? For nothing. She understood that she was much richer than she had been before, but she felt no joy in that. She would buy Peacock a house, give the rest of her fortune to charity, and perhaps enter a nunnery. Beautiful Sudonia was lost – she could remember only the good things about it, although, taking a bath, she did recall that this was much easier to do here than there – brilliant Waldo was no more, and Jonah . . . ?

Yes, what about him? She passed a worried night, and the next morning, early, she set off for his flat.

Fearfully, she rang his bell. He opened the door promptly. He was normally dressed.

'Hallo, Felicity!' he exclaimed. 'Hallo, darling!'

He took her in his arms and kissed her.

He knew that her first name was Felicity, having seen it on official documents, etc, but never before had he used it. Neither had he kissed her – or at least, not like this.

'You look marvellous!' he said, and kissed her again.

'You don't look so bad yourself,' she replied, flooded with relief and delight. 'The trip seems to have done you good.'

'Trip? What trip?'

She saw that he remembered nothing of Sudonia. Miranda, Sir Topas, Waldo – they were totally erased from his mind. They would be. They were a forgotten dream. All this she saw in a flash. She was glad she had not mentioned Sudonia by name, but she was at a loss for words.

He came to her aid unwittingly. 'I suppose you mean the show,' he said. *'Cinderella.* Done me good? I shouldn't think so. I seem to have brought one of their costumes home with me, by the way. God knows how I came by that. Done me good? Now you come to mention it, I feel terrific. All the better for seeing you, of course.' He kissed her again, with something of the mad movement of Waldo about him, but most tenderly (as a Sudonian would have put it) withal. 'Talking of props,' he said, 'that mirror's got knocked about a bit. Not that it matters. I've got no further use for it.'

'Jonah,' said Felicity tentatively, 'could we have some coffee?'

In her mind she had outlined a plan. Little by little,

tactfully, she would bring him to remember being struck by lightning on the slopes of the university campus, and persuade him that he had been knocked out of this world for a while. She had to, or else a lot of things would soon begin to puzzle him, including having jumped from mid-winter to spring.

But he was talking away, exuberantly, and she couldn't get a word in. 'You know,' he said, 'I've had enough of Sprockett's Electricals. What did I ever get from it, except a lot of money? Why don't we give it up? Get married and give it up?'

'Certainly, I'm all for it. Jonah, just listen – '

'We could leave it in capable hands. Plenty of those waiting to grab it! We've got plenty of money. We could spend it doing good works.'

'Yes, I've got a taste for good works. Er, Jonah – '

'And also,' said Jonah, waving his coffee spoon, 'I think it's time I got some education. Mine has been terribly one-sided. One of those Open University courses. What do you think?'

'Good idea. Jonah – '

It dawned on him that she was trying to break something to him, and he stopped in his tracks.

'Felicity, have I been ill?'

'Oh no, not exactly ill,' she replied, touched.

A grave expression invaded his happy face.

'M'm . . . I went to a psychiatrist, didn't I? . . . Yes, yes . . . Felicity, have I been locked up for a while?'

'No, you've been liberated.'

He laughed all over his face. 'Is that how you put it? Well, whatever they did, good for them, because I never felt better in my life.'

'You haven't got it quite right, darling . . .'

In small, tactful quantities, she brought back to him the story of the mirror, up to the point where they had

146

taken it to the university. It had been damaged by the lightning, she explained. It had lost its frame. Which was true. No need to tell him it had been damaged twice.

'Oh well,' he said cheerfully, 'it'll do to dress by, I suppose. Let's go and look at it.'

'No,' she said quickly.

'Oh come on. Afraid of disappearing? It's only a toy!'

Reluctantly, she followed him into his living room, where the mirror (concave or convex?) was propped against the wall. She hung back as he looked in it.

'No, it won't do to dress by,' he laughed. 'It distorts me! Look at this!'

In dread, she went and stood beside him. She was reflected as her radiant self, but the reflection that looked back at Jonah had straw-coloured hair and blazing blue eyes.

'I know hair can go white,' said Jonah, highly amused, 'but I didn't know it could go that colour!'

It was Waldo in the mirror. She had *known* he was up to something, giggling away to himself! She had *known* he had something up his sleeve! Or at least she should have known! Content to cease existing? With his IQ? Not he! He'd really pulled it off. He had come into this world with Jonah. He had come into this world *as* Jonah. He *was* Jonah. He was Jonah as he had always wanted himself to be.

'Funny,' said Jonah, '*you* look all right, but –'

'So do you.'

She hugged him as if she would never let him go. He disengaged himself and stared at her in an affectionately questioning way.

'I've got an idea you're humouring me, somehow. Have I really been ill?'

'You . . . you were not quite yourself, darling.'

147

'But – '

She felt an acute need to change the subject.

'What Open University course are you thinking of taking?'

'History and English Literature, I thought. I'd like to study the Middle Ages. You know, Age of Chaucer, sort of thing.'

'Yes,' said Felicity. 'Yes, I'm sure you'd be very good at it.'